DOCTOR WHO AND THE
KEEPER OF TRAKEN

DOCTOR WHO
AND THE
KEEPER OF TRAKEN

Based on the BBC television serial by Johnny Byrne by arrangement with the British Broadcasting Corporation

TERRANCE DICKS

Number 37 in the Dr Who Library

A TARGET BOOK
published by
the Paperback Division of
W. H. ALLEN & Co. PLC

A Target Book
Published in 1982
by the Paperback Division of W. H. Allen & Co. PLC
44 Hill Street, London W1X 8LB
Reprinted 1982 (twice)
Reprinted 1983
Reprinted 1984

Printed and bound in Great Britain by
Cox & Wyman Ltd, Reading

ISBN 0 426 20148 5

Contents

1

Escape to Danger

The Doctor had escaped.

Not for the first time, of course. In his many lives he had escaped from many dangers. But this was something special. This time he had escaped not from some monster's cave or tyrant's dungeon, but from a sort of pocket-sized parallel universe, called E-space.

Now the Doctor stood in his shirt-sleeves in the TARDIS control room, gazing at the crowded starscape on the big scanner screen.

Beside him was a smallish, round-faced, snub-nosed lad with an expression of cheerful impudence. This was Adric the only one of the Doctor's companions to make the journey back to N-space, the normal universe.

The Doctor's other companion, the Time Lady Romana, had decided to stay in E-space, pursuing her crusade against the slavery that had angered and revolted her. Perhaps that was what Romana had always needed, mused the Doctor, a cause to devote herself to whole-heartedly. She had never been really happy as a footloose wanderer through time and space. At least she had K9 to help her. The Doctor smiled at the thought of the oddly-assorted duo: the cool sophisticated Time Lady and the opinionated little computer in the shape of a robot dog. They made a formidable combination.

Adric's voice interrupted the Doctor's thoughts. 'So this is N-space?'

The Doctor studied the star-filled screen with satisfaction. 'The old home universe! It's many times larger than the one you're used to, of course.'

'All those stars! Do you really know them all?'

'Only the interesting ones!'

'How can you tell which is which?'

'Oh, you know,' said the Doctor vaguely, 'probability theory, that sort of thing.' He frowned at the screen. 'I can't quite see how we've ended up in this neighbourhood, though. We're supposed to be returning to Gallifrey. Oh, well ...' The Doctor shrugged. Pin-point accuracy had never been a feature of the TARDIS navigational systems.

'I don't see how probability theory comes into it!' said Adric.

The Doctor looked thoughtfully at him. Adric was naturally shrewd, and he'd learned a great deal since becoming the Doctor's companion. Some of his questions were becoming disturbingly acute. 'Now see here, Adric. I give you a privileged glimpse into the mystery of time, open your mind to adventure beyond imagining—and you have the audacity to criticise my logic?'

'All I'm saying is a lot of what you say doesn't actually make much sense.'

'Oh, you've noticed that have you? Well, as long as that's understood, you and I are going to get on splendidly!'

Adric returned his attention to the screen. 'Where are we, anyway?'

'Somewhere in the region of Mettula Orionsis, I should say. Does that make sense?'

Adric studied the navigational console. 'Well, it's

what it says here.'

'You're starting to get the hang of that console.' The Doctor touched a control, narrowing the display on the screen to a particular star-cluster. 'That's the Traken Union—famous for its universal harmony. A whole empire held together by ...' The Doctor paused, groping for some way to express the incredibly complex bio-electronic structure that united the Traken Empire.

'Held together by ...'

'Well?'

'Just by people being terribly nice to each other!'

'That makes a change.'

'Mind you, I haven't actually been there . . . as far as I can remember. I just know it by repute.'

'Is that why we're going there now?'

'Going to Traken? Who says so?'

'You've set the controls to take us there.'

The Doctor looked down at the console. 'You mean you set them.'

'No, I assumed you did.'

'But I didn't, did I?' said the Doctor thoughtfully. 'Now, I wonder what probability theory would have to say about that!'

The Doctor went over to the big old-fashioned hatstand that stood incongruously beside the console. It held a long flowing coat, an incredibly long scarf and a hat with a broad floppy brim. The Doctor took down the coat and slipped into it, nearly upsetting the hatstand in the process. 'Why does this thing always wobble?' he muttered indignantly. 'You stick a book under one leg, then you need a book under the next one and so on, round and round, doing all the legs in turn. It's perfectly infuriating.'

Adric was busy at the console. 'Doctor, there's

something wrong with the controls!'

'What? Oh, yes, well there would be.' The Doctor went over to join him. 'What's the problem?'

'They seem to be operating themselves! As far as I can make out, we've gone into orbit round one of those planets.'

The Doctor studied the console, and nodded thoughtfully. 'I thought so!'

'You thought what?'

'I thought you might appreciate it if I appeared to be in control of the situation. I mean, we could always panic, I suppose, but where would that get us?'

Adric was beginning to panic already. 'But what's happening?'

'I haven't the faintest idea.'

'You're supposed to know these things. You're a Time Lord, aren't you?'

'My dear Adric, if I knew what was going to happen all the time there'd be no fun in anything—' The Doctor broke off, staring over Adric's shoulder. 'Hello!'

Adric whirled round. A kind of golden throne had appeared in the TARDIS Huddled back in its velvety black lining was an incredibly old man. He wore a high-collared golden robe with an ornate stripe down the sleeves. His face was wrinkled like a winter-stored apple, and he had a high, bald forehead and a straggling white beard. He looked frail, almost emaciated, except for his eyes, which blazed with intelligence and life.

'How do you do, Doctor?' The voice, too, was old and feeble, but there was a thread of vitality in it that matched the eyes.

Adric stared at the apparition in horror. The Doctor put a reassuring hand on his shoulder. 'It's all right, Adric, keep calm. This, I imagine is the Keeper of Traken.'

10

'Well guessed, Doctor,' said the ancient voice. 'It appears that the reports of your intelligence are true.'

'Oh, it wasn't difficult,' said the Doctor modestly. 'There can't be many people in the Universe with the power to take control of the TARDIS. And as for just dropping in like this ...'

'You're taking it all very calmly,' whispered Adric. 'What's going on?'

'Time reveals all, Adric,' said the Doctor, hoping that it would. He turned to their strange visitor. 'Well, Keeper, how can I help you?'

The Keeper paused for a moment, gathering his strength. 'Listen closely, Doctor. As you see, the passing ages have taken their toll.'

'I know the feeling!'

'The time of my Dissolution is near, and the power entrusted to me is ebbing away.'

'Your powers are still fairly impressive,' said the Doctor drily. 'I couldn't flit around in an old chair like that!'

'I have all the minds of the Union to draw on. I am only the organising principle.' The Keeper paused. 'It is in the name of that Union that I ask you to come to Traken.'

'Well ...' said the Doctor dubiously.

'You do well to hesitate, Doctor. Think carefully before you agree. There is great danger, for you and for your companion.'

The Doctor brightened, intrigued rather than discouraged by the promise of danger. 'How so, Keeper?'

'I fear our beloved world of Traken faces disaster.'

Adric gave the Doctor a sceptical look. 'I thought you said they lived in universal harmony.'

'Sssh!' said the Doctor, but the Keeper had overheard.

11

'The Doctor has not exaggerated. Since the time of the first Keeper, our Union has indeed been the most harmonious in the Universe.' He looked at the Doctor in mild surprise. 'Does the boy not know that?'

'He's not ... local,' said the Doctor hurriedly. 'Not from these parts.'

Adric blinked.

Suddenly the Keeper was somewhere else, his throne just in front of the TARDIS scanner screen. 'How vain one can be! I thought the whole Universe knew the history of our little Empire.'

Adric looked puzzled and the Doctor said, 'It really is an extraordinary place, Traken. They say the atmosphere of goodness is so strong that evil just shrivels up and dies.' He grinned. 'Perhaps that's why I've never been there!'

'Rumour does not exaggerate,' said the Keeper solemnly.

Adric gasped. 'Look, Doctor!'

The Doctor turned. A picture had appeared on the TARDIS scanner screen. It showed an ornamental garden tended by cheerful, broad-shouldered men in grey working-clothes and high boots. They were raking paths, tending flower-beds, potting plants—all the many activities that go to the maintenance of a successful garden.

'These are the Fosters,' said the Keeper. 'The garden they tend symbolises the spiritual welfare of our Union.' He gazed for a moment at the peaceful scene. 'Nevertheless, sometimes they are visited by evil.'

The picture changed, to show the planet Traken seen from some vantage point in deep space. A spot of fiercely burning crimson light was streaking meteor-like towards it.

The picture changed back to the garden, and

12

suddenly the crimson fireball streaked through the air and buried itself in a flower-bed. The crimson glow faded to reveal a fearsome and terrifying creature. Immensely tall and powerful, with broad shoulders, long arms and a fearsomely scowling, sculptured head, it looked rather like an alien being in some kind of space armour—though it was hard to be sure whether it really was armour or the creature's natural shape, since it was still surrounded by the fiery crimson glow. The Fosters seemed more curious than alarmed. One of two went over to look at the strange being, but most simply got on with their gardening.

'They don't seem very worried,' whispered Adric.

The Keeper's wrinkled old face broke into a smile. 'The Fosters know there is little to fear from these visitations, though perhaps they regret the interruption to their gardening. They named this creature "Melkur".'

The Doctor frowned. 'Melkur?'

'Literally, "a fly caught by honey".'

Adric saw the towering monster on the screen give a kind of convulsive start, as if striving desperately to move. Then, slowly it froze into immobility, the radiant sheen fading from the mighty limbs. Finally it became quite still—as still as some great statue carved in stone. The watching Fosters drifted back to their work.

The picture changed. A high stone wall had been built, so that the statue now stood in a sizeable walled garden of its own. The whole area was a jungle of weeds and shrubs and bushes.

'What will become of this Melkur, Keeper?' asked the Doctor curiously.

'Its baleful influence will not extend beyond the place that has been set aside for it. It is called the Grove. And even there it will only produce a few extra weeds.'

13

The Doctor and Adric saw that the Melkur was frozen in place like a garden statue. There was even moss growing on the terrifying shape.

The Keeper said, 'Like others before it, the creature will calcify, and pass harmlessly into the soil. But the death of any living creature is painful to us. Even the Melkur is cared for.'

They saw a young red-headed girl in a flowing blue dress approaching the Melkur. She carried a bunch of red flowers which she laid at the Melkur's feet. 'And how are you today, you poor Melkur?' she said. 'My name is Kassia. The Fosters have appointed me to look after you, but there isn't very much I can do. It must be awful to be rooted to the spot like a tree.' She looked up at the statue, almost as if expecting some sign of life. The grim features stared impassively back down at her. 'If you weren't so evil you might be able to move around a little, just inside the Grove. But being so wicked, you can't even speak! Never mind, I'll come and see you again soon.' She turned and walked away, and they saw her disappear through a massive iron gate.

The Doctor said, 'That particular evil seems to be well under control.'

'Seemed, Doctor,' corrected the Keeper sternly. 'The events you have been watching happened many years ago. Young Kassia is now grown up. Indeed such was her purity of spirit that she was chosen to be a Consul. She is married now, to her fellow Consul, Tremas. Somehow I sensed that the day of her wedding was to be a turning point for Traken ...'

Now there was another picture on the screen. It showed an enormous circular council-chamber with ornately carved and decorated stone walls. The high-arched roof was supported by huge pillars. One

14

side of the hall was dominated by a set of massive doors, the other by a strange dome-like structure walled in some transparent material. Inside could be seen a great throne, like the one in which the Keeper now sat in the TARDIS. Above the throne there burned a golden flame. The whole structure was raised above the level of the rest of the room by a kind of dais, with a short flight of steps leading up to it. On a nearby wall was a display of energy-weapons—hand-blasters and energy-rifles—arranged like trophies.

Before the dais there stood a group of colourfully dressed figures. They wore rich velvet robes in many different colours—blue and black and red and green— and over these they wore high-collared golden cloaks. They wore heavy gold chains of office around their necks. These were the five Consuls, rulers of the Traken Union. Silver goblets brimming with wine were in their hands and they were in a festive mood, celebrating the wedding of two of their fellow Consuls. Scattered groups of Fosters and other citizens stood drinking and talking at a respectful distance.

Watching, the Doctor reflected that a wedding was a wedding, anywhere in the galaxy. The same jokes, the same roars of laughter, the same good wishes and congratulations, and, inevitably the same cries of 'Speech! Speech!'

In response to these cries, a tall impressive-looking man went to the foot of the steps, holding up his hands for silence. He was somewhere in his forties with a strong, handsome face, his brown hair and beard streaked with grey. Presumably this was the bridegroom, Tremas. 'Enough, fellow Trakens, enough! Applause is heady stuff and I've already drunk more wine than is fitting for a man of my responsibilities. To be a Consul and father to Nyssa here carries duties

15

enough—' He took the hand of a slender brown-haired girl. 'But to be a husband once again, and to Kassia!'

There was a roar of laughter and applause.

A tall red-haired woman stepped forward and took Tremas's other hand. 'My husband is right—the wine has flowed freely tonight. Perhaps I should take him home!'

The Doctor saw that this was the same girl who had placed flowers at the foot of the Melkur. She was now several years older, sophisticated and strikingly beautiful, and wore the robes of a Consul with a becoming dignity.

One of the Consuls, a tall thin-faced man said, 'Already you begin to pamper him, Kassia, just as you do that Melkur of yours in the Grove!'

A woman Consul, old and white-haired said, 'People had begun to think she was married to the Melkur, all these years she's been tending him!'

Another Consul, jolly and round-faced, with a fringe of beard said, 'Poor Melkur! I hope Tremas fares better than Melkur under Kassia's care! The poor monster's covered in moss!'

There was a shout of laughter—but Kassia didn't seem to find any of this funny. 'I am sure it does not become us to mock the Melkur,' she said frostily.

Behind her an old voice said, 'I rather think it is you they are mocking, Kassia!'

They all turned to see that the wizened figure of the Keeper had materialised on his throne. The transparent casing of the dome slid back so they could approach him.

Tremas bowed low. 'Keeper! I am honoured that you were able to join us.'

'No affairs of state could keep me away from an occasion such as this.' The Keeper held out his hands. 'Come, both of you. Receive my blessing.'

16

Kassia too bowed her head. 'As my husband says, we are honoured, Keeper.'

They came forward to the head of the steps and the wizened old figure smiled benignly down at them. 'As I recall, Kassia promised to tend the Melkur while it still lived. Who would have thought its passing would be so protracted? Kassia has fulfilled her duties loyally, and we now release her.'

Kassia stared at him in consternation, almost as if it did not please her to be released from her long task.

'Come, Kassia,' said Tremas gently. 'Thank the Keeper.'

Kassia stared wildly at him. 'But who will tend him? Who will tend Melkur?'

'The Fosters, perhaps,' said the Keeper. 'Since you drove them from the Grove it has become neglected.' He held out his hands and Tremas and Kassia came forward.

The Keeper looked from one to the other and then pointed with a skinny hand. 'You, Nyssa, come here.'

Reluctantly, Nyssa came to stand between her father and his new wife.

The Keeper said, 'Nyssa shall watch over your Melkur, Kassia. And she must share in the blessing too,' He beckoned them forward and they knelt at his feet. In his high, quavering voice the Keeper said, 'Nearing the time of my Dissolution, I bless the marriage of these two, Tremas and Kassia, truest of my Consuls, together with Nyssa, now daughter to them both.'

The Keeper looked round the assembly. 'And now I have news for you. The time has come for the naming of my successor. Consul Tremas, I have chosen you!' The picture on the screen faded and the Keeper's voice with it.

In the TARDIS, the Doctor and Adric turned to

look at the same wizened figure on the throne.

The Keeper said, 'What you have seen occurred just a short time ago. Now begins the time of my Dissolution. No Keeper lasts forever, and the time of transition is always difficult. But even as I named Tremas my successor I sensed . . .' the old voice trailed off.

'Sensed what, Keeper?' said the Doctor gently.

'Evil! All-pervading evil, somehow nurtured in those three good people, standing before me to share my blessing. My time is short, Doctor, and I need your help.'

'Well, anything we can do, of course . . .'

'Me too,' said Adric, curiously touched by the old Keeper's appeal.

The Keeper stared at Adric, the eyes burning in the wrinkled face. 'I am reluctant to involve you. Indeed, I am fearful even to involve the Doctor. He will face unimaginable hazards, confront power that could obliterate even a Time Lord.' He turned to the Doctor. 'Take care, my friend. Thank you . . . and farewell.'

As suddenly as he had come, the Keeper disappeared.

2

Melkur Wakes

The Doctor seemed to accept the Keeper's departure
quite calmly. 'Well, Adric?'
'Well what?'
'What do you make of it all?'
'Seems a funny way of going about things.'
The Doctor was busy at the console.
'What are you doing, Doctor?'
'Preparing for an unobtrusive landing on Traken.
Don't want to calcify like poor old Melkur, do we?'
'I hope we know what we're doing.'
'So do I ... What do you mean—we?'
'All right,' said Adric placatingly. 'You!'

The council-chamber doors gave first onto an anteroom, then onto a high-walled courtyard. The doors
were flanked with huge, leafy plants in big stone urns,
and the whole courtyard was colourful with plants and
vines and flowers, their rich scents hanging heavy on
the warm night air. Light streamed through the doors
as the last of the wedding guests came out of the
anteroom in chattering groups and made their way
home.

Tremas was among the last to leave, and he stood for
a moment gazing up into the night sky ablaze with
stars. 'If all the stars were silver, and the sky a giant

purse in my fist, I couldn't be happier than I am tonight!'

Close behind Tremas came Neman, a stocky, broad-shouldered man with a heavy moustache, Neman was a Proctor, the official in charge of the Fosters. He looked at Tremas with a certain wariness. 'Poetry apart, Consul Tremas, I'd sooner be rich than Keeper-Nominate, any night of the year.'

Tremas made no reply. The news that he had been chosen as the Keeper's successor was not entirely unexpected. Yet somehow the formal announcement had come as a considerable shock. Tremas's reactions were mixed, to say the least. To be Keeper-Nominate and then Keeper was a tremendous honour, the highest on Traken. Yet at the same time, the responsibilities of the office were a crushing burden. With the aid of the Source, the Keeper thought and felt for all the Traken Empire. He acquired such knowledge and such power that he was scarcely human. His concern was not with any single individual, but with all the millions of souls that made up the Empire. To his friends and, above all, to his family, he was lost.

In his heart, Tremas knew that the Keeper had virtually ended his second marriage at the moment he had blessed it. As the announcement was made, he had caught Kassia's eye, and saw that she too was fully aware of what must come.

Tremas forced a smile. 'I wasn't thinking of state duties, Proctor Neman.'

Neman beamed. 'Of course—Kassia! She should be with you, surely?'

'She has gone to the Grove, to take leave of her precious Melkur.'

Nyssa had appeared in the doorway behind them. 'Aren't you jealous, father?'

20

Tremas made no reply.

Neman laughed and said, 'His happiness is like the stars, he says. There's plenty to share with everyone—even Melkur!'

The grove was dark, silent except for the wind rustling the bushes.

Kassia stood staring up at Melkur, her face pale and streaked with tears. She was talking to the great statue as if to some old friend. 'So Tremas is Keeper-Nominate. They all think it a great honour. But when the Keeper's time of Dissolution comes and Tremas becomes Keeper, he will be taken from me forever.' She looked up at Melkur, tears streaming down her face. 'And that time will be soon. I know it will be soon.'

The savage mask of Melkur's face stared down at her. Kassia heard a voice, a voice so faint that it seemed audible only in her mind. 'Soon ... the time will be soon. I can help you, Kassia.'

The Doctor staggered into the TARDIS control room carrying two enormous dusty volumes.

Adric looked up. 'What have you got there?'

'Knowledge,' said the Doctor impressively. 'The accumulated wisdom of centuries. In other words, a couple of my old Time Logs.' He dropped the volumes onto the console, and began leafing through them. 'You see, it's possible that I have visited Traken before. It's so hard to keep track.'

'You find it helps, do you, keeping a Time Log. A kind of diary?'

'Well, it used to. I'm afraid I haven't really kept it up. Far too busy these days. These may not even be the right volumes.' He heaved one of them up and passed it over to Adric. 'Here, you try this one.'

Adric's knees buckled under the weight of the massive tome. He set it down on the floor and opened it. 'What am I supposed to be looking for?'

'Oh, you know—Traken, Keepers, All-Pervading Evil ...'

'Universal Harmony?'

'That's right. Anything along those lines.'

Adric turned to the back page. 'There isn't even an index!'

'Life doesn't have an index, Adric,' said the Doctor magnificently. 'Now hush, I need to concentrate.'

The old Foster had left the wedding party early—the noise and the laughter had been too much for him, and he decided to work in the soothing calm of the Grove. Not that you could do any proper gardening there, of course. With that Melkur thing there, the place was no better than a jungle. Still, he could tidy it up a bit ... He was working in the clearing that held Melkur when some strange sensation made him look up. The statue-like figure loomed dark and menacing above him. He had the strangest feeling that it was watching him.

Drawn by some strange fascination, the old man straightened his back and drew closer. He stared up at the harsh, brooding face with its staring, blank eye-sockets—and suddenly they were blank no longer. They were alive, glowing redly. With a cry of fear, the old man staggered back, transfixed by the fiery, burning gaze.

The body was found the following morning, by some of

22

the Fosters who had come looking for the old man. They reported it to Proctor Neman, who in turn informed the Consuls.

Soon Consul Seron, a tall austere-looking man, was kneeling over the body, watched by Proctor Neman and the round-faced Consul Luvic, his usually cheerful features now grave and concerned.

Seron straightened up. 'Kassia has called a meeting, you say?'

'Apparently! More of her strange ideas, it seems.'

Seron beckoned to the Fosters, who wrapped the frail old body in a shroud and carried it gently away. 'Kassia is a gifted sensitive, her spiritual qualities beyond all doubt.' He smiled. 'However, Tremas has yet to persuade her that we live in a rational world, not in some chaos of superstition.'

Relieved, Luvic said, 'So the death was natural?'

'He was full of years,' said Seron gently. 'Old men die, even here.'

Neman said gruffly, 'With respect, Consul, I've never seen one die like that. The pain on his face ... the fear ... Is that natural?'

'Unusual certainly,' said Seron judiciously. 'But we must not leap to conclusions.' He glanced at the nearby Fosters and lowered his voice. 'Particularly in the presence of others. There is rumour enough abroad on Traken. At such time as this ...'

The approaching Dissolution of a Keeper always brought unrest to the usually peaceful Union of Traken. Strange rumours swept through the uneasy populace ...

Neman too lowered his voice. 'All this restlessness in the Union, Consul ... Perhaps the Fosters should be armed again?'

Luvic gave him a look of alarm. 'Armed? An unusual

suggestion! The Fosters have not been armed for generations.'

'These are unusual times, Consul,' said Neman bluntly.

Tremas approached, frowning at a portable energy-scanner in his hand.

'Well, Tremas,' said Seron with a kind of forced cheerfulness, 'has science brought us any nearer to discovering how the Foster died?'

Tremas said gravely, 'It's fantastic. So fantastic that I don't know what to believe.'

Seron raised an eyebrow. 'Fantastic?'

'I've scanned the whole area several times. The readings are very strange.' He handed the instrument to Seron. 'See for yourself.'

Seron studied the instrument for a moment and then turned to Luvic. 'It seems our worst fears are confirmed.'

'They are?' asked Luvic worriedly.

Seron smiled. 'Yes, it seems Tremas has fallen under Kassia's spell in more ways than one. She has infected him with her irrational fears.' He drew Luvic aside. 'Tell the meeting I shall be delayed for a moment or two. Clearly our friend Tremas needs humouring.'

Relieved, Luvic bustled away.

As soon as he was out of earshot, Seron turned back to Tremas, his face grave. 'These readings—what do they mean?'

'Impossible to say. They were produced by an energy source beyond the scope of the instrument to analyse or measure.'

'Could it be some error? The scanner has not been used for many years. Perhaps it is faulty.'

'An error? A fault in the instrument? Yes, it could be.' There was no conviction in Tremas's voice.

'And if the readings are true?'

'If the readings are true,' said Tremas slowly. 'Some force, some immensely powerful, unknown force has arrived on Traken.'

Adric looked up from the bulky volume and sighed.

'Fascinating stuff, isn't it?' said the Doctor cheerfully.

'If only I could understand it.'

'What do you mean?'

'Look,' said Adric despairingly. 'I read about something you've done, and then over the page the same event hasn't happened at all. Another page, and you say it really did happen, but a very long time ago.'

'I suppose it's all a bit above your head,' said the Doctor tolerantly. 'Mind you, they say I have a very sophisticated prose style.'

'And as for your handwriting!'

'What about my handwriting?'

'It's marvellous,' said Adric hurriedly.

Suddenly he stared over the Doctor's shoulder, his eyes widening. The Doctor turned, following Adric's gaze.

The central column of the TARDIS was no longer rising and falling—which meant that the TARDIS had landed.

There was a rather uneasy silence.

'Well, we've arrived,' said the Doctor.

'Yes.'

The Doctor switched on the scanner screen. 'Let's see what the place really looks like.'

The screen showed a kind of enclosed garden, filled with overgrown flower-beds and trailing vines. The place seemed absolutely crammed with luxuriant foliage, and there was something curiously sinister about it.

Thoughtfully, the Doctor studied the scene. 'Just the spot if you were in the mood for a bit of gardening. Ever hear of Capability Brown?' He reached for hat and scarf.

'Murder?' said old Katura incredulously. 'Here, in the precincts of the Court?'

All five Consuls were gathered in the Sanctum. Two Fosters stood by the door.

Tremas said, 'We do not know that it was murder, Consul Katura.'

'You have determined the cause of death?'

'Surely it was natural?' interrupted Luvic, looking appealingly at Seron.

Tremas was about to answer when Seron said warningly, 'We must not be alarmist.'

Tremas chose his words carefully. 'The old Foster died through contact with some high-energy source. How and why it happened—we cannot say.'

'A sign,' whispered Kassia, almost to herself. 'The power of Melkur.' She rose, raising her voice. 'Consuls, I sense some danger coming to us all. The Fosters must be armed.' She indicated the display of energy-weapons on the walls of the Sanctum, weapons which had been little more than showpieces for generations.

Seron frowned. 'With all due respect to your intuition, Kassia, we cannot allow superstition to stampede reason.'

'I have my reasons!'

'Then you have only to let the Consuls know what they are.'

Kassia was silent.

'Well, Kassia?' said Tremas gently.

Kassia looked hopelessly back at him, unable to explain or justify the terrible foreboding of evil that had come over her. If she told him Melkur had spoken, he would think she was mad ...

Seron's voice was calm and reasonable. 'We are the Keeper's appointed Consuls, Kassia. Let us be guided by his benevolent wisdom, not by our own irrational fears and intuitions.'

'Then let us summon the Keeper,' said Kassia passionately. 'Let him decide what must be done.'

'We have no right to disturb him at this time ...'

For all his fussiness, there was a streak of obstinacy in Luvic. He sensed there was something wrong, and he had no intention of letting Seron over-ride him. 'First we must decide on the question of arming the Fosters. I feel that Kassia may well be right on that point. They should be armed. After all, it can do no harm. I should like a vote.'

Seron looked around the little group of Consuls. One by one they nodded in assent. Seron beckoned to one of the Fosters at the door. 'Send for Proctor Neman.'

The Doctor's original plan was that he should go out and explore, while Adric stayed in the TARDIS—a plan to which Adric objected violently. After a certain amount of wrangling, it was agreed that Adric should accompany the Doctor for the first part of the exploration. The Doctor operated the door control and they stepped out of the TARDIS into the overgrown garden. The dense vegetation crowded round the little clearing in which they'd landed. Facing them was what looked like an enormous statue of some

27

armoured figure. They stood looking up at it and it seemed to glare balefully back at them.

'There he is,' said the Doctor. 'Melkur!'

Adric shivered. 'It feels almost—alive.'

The Doctor rapped the statue disrespectfully with his knuckles. 'Feels pretty well calcified to me!'

'I get a nasty feeling it's watching us.'

'The fresh air's probably going to your head,' said the Doctor solemnly. 'All that being cooped up in the TARDIS, bound to have an effect.'

They followed a stone-flagged path, trees and plants rustling eerily all around them. The path led them to a high wall in which was set a massive wrought-iron gate. It was firmly closed.

Adric looked up at the Doctor. 'Now what?'

'I'm going on through the gate. You can go back to the TARDIS, you've had your look around.'

'Oh no, I'm not. I'm coming with you.'

'Not a step further,' said the Doctor firmly. 'Go on, off you go. Finish reading the Time Logs or something.'

The Doctor pushed the right-hand side of the gate. It refused to budge. He put his shoulder to it and heaved. Still nothing.

Adric slipped nimbly past the Doctor, and tugged at the gate. It was unlocked and slid smoothly open. Adric slipped through.

'Hey!' shouted the Doctor and hurried after him.

They found themselves in a courtyard, facing a squad of burly, grey-clad men with blasters in their hands.

'Ah good, the welcoming committee,' said the Doctor cheerfully. 'How do you do?'

Levelling their blasters, the little group surrounded

them in a menacing semi-circle.

'I wonder what we've done this time?' said the Doctor, and raised his hands.

3

Intruders

In the Keeper's Sanctum the stormy Council meeting was still in progress. Kassia was on her feet. 'I speak for the people of the Traken Union. They ask why the crops fail, why drought or floods disturb our planets. What are we to tell them?'

Calm and reasonable as always, Seron said, 'Such events are normal when the span of a Keeper nears its end.'

'Nothing can be normal at such a time. The Keeper whose protection we have enjoyed for a thousand years is dying, his power grows weaker day by day . . .' Kassia was almost frantic in her urgency.

Tremas tried to calm her 'Traken has survived such times as this before. We can do so again, with the help of science and understanding.'

'Fine words, husband—but no great comfort to a people who feel themselves being stripped of their traditional protections.'

'The Keeper knows our situation,' said Seron obstinately. 'We must leave him to deal with it as he thinks best.'

'No,' said Kassia passionately. 'We cannot afford to wait, to stand on ceremony. We must summon the Keeper. I propose that we put it to a vote.'

'I agree,' said Luvic. 'The sooner the better.'

As Keeper-Nominate, this was Tremas's responsibility. He looked round the group. 'Very well. You all know the law. The vote must be unanimous.' His voice became formal. 'Consuls of Traken it is proposed that we summon the Keeper. All those in favour will raise their hands.'

One by one the hands went up—all except Seron's.

'Consul Seron?' said Tremas.

'Since the majority are agreed, then I will concur,' said Seron and raised his hand.

The deep clangour of a warning bell filled the Sanctum. 'It appears that something more important than our business here has occurred,' said Seron drily.

The doors opened and the Doctor and Adric were marched in by a band of armed Fosters, led by Proctor Neman. 'Consuls, we have found the source of the evil,' announced Neman proudly.

Tremas looked at the two strange figures in astonishment. 'Who are you?'

'I hate to say this,' said the Doctor plaintively. 'But I'm really not very impressed with Traken hospitality.'

'*Who are you?*'

Adric felt the tenseness in the atmosphere and decided a few straight answers might serve them better. 'I'm Adric,' he said brightly. 'And this is the Doctor. We've just arrived.'

'I'm sure it's only the usual misunderstanding,' said the Doctor, airily. 'We keep running into this sort of thing. But this time we were actually invited here. You know, asked to pitch in, help out, that sort of thing!'

'Who asked you here?'

'Well, I hate name-dropping,' said the Doctor, obviously enjoying the whole thing tremendously, 'but as a matter of fact it was the Keeper.'

Tremas leaned forward urgently. 'You have had contact with the Keeper?'

31

'In a manner of speaking, yes.'

'The Keeper said someone would come to help Traken. Are you the one, Doctor?'

'Well, unless the Keeper makes a habit of asking strangers for help ...'

Kassia looked outraged. 'Our sacred law decrees that the Keeper speaks only through his Consuls.'

Seron, as always, did his best to apply logic to the situation. 'How did you arrive here, Doctor? In some kind of space-craft, I presume?'

The Doctor nodded. 'We landed in a sort of walled garden, close to a big, rather sinister-looking statue.'

Seron looked at his fellow Consuls. 'The Grove.'

'We thought we'd walk the rest of the way,' explained the Doctor. 'Get a bit of fresh air, stretch our legs, that kind of thing.'

'Then your craft will still be there—in the Grove?'

'I imagine so.'

'Proctor Neman, send some of your Fosters to confirm this.'

'At once, Consul.' Beckoning to a couple of Fosters to follow him, Neman hurried away.

In the Grove, the eyes of Melkur began glowing red. They glowed brigher and brighter, until suddenly twin beams of light lanced out, enveloping the TARDIS in a fiery radiance. The TARDIS vanished.

Minutes later Neman and his Fosters entered the Grove and began their search. They found nothing strange or new. There was only the giant brooding statue of Melkur.

The Grove was small and the search did not take long.

Before long, Neman was back in the Sanctum, delivering his report. 'There was nothing there, Consuls. No alien craft of any kind.'

'Perhaps I should have warned you,' said the Doctor. 'It doesn't look very much like a space-craft. More like a tall blue box, you could easily have missed it.'

'There was nothing,' repeated Neman stubbornly. 'No alien object of any kind. Apart from Melkur, the Grove was empty.'

The Doctor looked down at Adric. 'Funny, I could have sworn we brought the TARDIS!'

'They are lying to us,' said Kassia fiercely. 'Does anybody doubt it?'

'Why don't you just summon the Keeper?' suggested the Doctor. 'He'll confirm what I say—and save an awful lot of fuss into the bargain.'

'The summoning of the Keeper has already been decided upon,' said Tremas stiffly. 'Fellow Consuls?'

All five Consuls rose and went to the transparent walled Chamber at the far end of the Sanctum. There was a complex control panel at the foot of the dais, and the Consuls knelt before it.

Each Consul wore a jewelled ring, and one by one they inserted the ring jewels into key-slots in the base of the panel.

The Doctor and Adric watched interestedly. 'What's going on?' whispered Adric.

'Some sort of security arrangement, I suppose. Obviously, they all have to be present to call the old chap.'

In the Grove the eyes of Melkur glowed red. The great head turned stiffly, looking towards the gate. The head tilted a little, as if listening.

Slowly Melkur came to life. It took a step, then

33

another. Like a walking statue, the huge figure stumbled towards the gate.

Their preparations complete, the five Consuls rose, drawing back a little from the dais.

Tremas raised his voice in a formal chant. 'Keeper of Traken! By unanimous consent, your Consuls summon you.'

For a moment nothing happened.

Then the fountain of flame above the throne burned brighter, higher—and the figure of the old Keeper materialised in the chair.

The transparent walls of the Chamber slid back.

The Keeper sat slumped in his chair, looking incredibly old and weary. 'Why do you summon me?'

'We have strangers among us, Keeper,' said Tremas. 'They claim that they are known to you.'

'They even dare to say that they come to Traken at your request,' added Kassia fiercely.

'Bring them forward,' said the Keeper wearily.

The Doctor and Adric were urged forward until they stood before the Keeper at the base of the dais.

Adric was shocked at the extent to which the Keeper had aged, even since they had last seen him. He looked older and more feeble than ever, his head slumped on his chest, his eyes half closed. The Doctor raised his voice. 'Sorry to trouble you, Keeper, but we seem to have a bit of a misunderstanding here!'

The attention of everyone in the Sanctum was concentrated on the Keeper. No one saw the main door of the Sanctum was slowly opening. In the gap appeared the towering figure of Melkur, glowing red eyes fixed on the weary figure on the throne.

The Doctor spoke again. 'Please, Keeper! Tell them who we are!'

34

The Keeper's head jerked upright. His eyes opened wide, looking, though no one realised it, not at the Doctor but past him, transfixed by the burning eyes of the massive figure that lurked in the shadows behind the partly open door.

'Evil!' gasped the Keeper. 'The Sanctum is invaded!'

'Keeper, please!' called the Doctor. 'Tell them!'

The Keeper's face twisted with horror. 'Consuls, we are invaded! Evil ... infinite evil ...'

The wizened figure of the Keeper slumped back on the throne, and faded away.

The Consuls turned accusingly towards the Doctor, and the Fosters moved forwards, their blasters levelled.

4

The Voice of Melkur

Protestingly, the Doctor raised his hands. 'You're about to make a very serious mistake. I can see you're all charming, reasonable people at heart. The least you can do is hear what we have to say.'

'Execute them!' snapped Kassia. 'Evil must be stamped out.'

'I quite agree,' said the Doctor. 'And Adric and I are ready to stamp with the best of them. But let's stamp with some justice, with precision.' He looked around the little group. 'Consuls, surely you can see what happened here? The Keeper was attacked by some kind of hostile force.'

Consul Seron waved the Fosters back. 'Do you imply that one of us used such a force against the Keeper?' It was clear that the very thought was horrifying to him.

'Someone here, or someone very close!'

Katura was equally appalled. 'One of us—against the Keeper?'

'But who would dare do such a thing?' asked Luvic plaintively.

Kassia glared fiercely at the Doctor and Adric. 'It is useless to lie. The Keeper recognised you for what you are—creatures of Melkur!'

'Melkur?' said Tremas sharply.

'Of course. The evil originates from him. Surely you

all realise?' Kassia's voice rose in hysteria. 'The evil is before you, before your eyes ...'

Her face twisted with anguish, she covered her eyes with her hands and collapsed sobbing to the ground.

Emotional displays were unknown in the Sanctum and there was immediate confusion and consternation.

Tremas and old Katura lifted Kassia gently to her feet, and Luvic hurried forward with a chair.

They settled her into it, and Tremas stood back, looking on helplessly as Katura knelt beside his wife, clasping her hands and talking to her in a low, soothing voice.

He turned and looked almost apologetically at the Doctor. 'My wife is unwell ... There have been many problems of late, much strain ...'

The Doctor said thoughtfully, 'She believes Melkur is the source of the evil?'

'She is obsessed with the creature,' said Seron. 'Even though it is now no more than a statue.'

Luvic said, 'It all began when she was a child. She used to take it flowers.'

The Doctor nodded, remembering the pictures the Keeper had shown them on the TARDIS scanner screen. 'Tell me more about Melkur. Has it shown any signs of life, of activity? Has anything strange or unusual happened?'

Tremas said slowly, 'There was the death of the Foster ...' He told the Doctor about the old man who had been found dead at the Melkur's feet.

Seron said sceptically, 'Doctor, are you suggesting that the Foster was killed and the Keeper attacked by some kind of supernatural force?'

'Not in the least. A high-energy beam, more likely.' The Doctor began patting his pockets. 'Now if only I had the right kind of scanner ...'

Tremas produced a small black instrument from beneath his robes. 'Something like this, perhaps?'

'Just the thing,' said the Doctor delightedly. He took the little device from Tremas and studied it absorbedly.

'You are a scientist, Doctor?'

The Doctor nodded. 'And so I see are you, Consul Tremas. Been investigating high-energy force fields, eh?'

'You are familiar with bioelectronics, Doctor?' It was rare for Tremas to encounter a fellow scientist. So many of the problems of Traken were taken care of by the power of the Source that the sciences had been somewhat neglected. Tremas's interest in such matters was regarded as a harmless eccentricity.

'Oh, I've dabbled a little,' said the Doctor modestly.

Tremas looked round at his fellow Consuls. 'If the Court will permit an exchange of scientific views, I believe that the Doctor may be able to assist me.'

Katura was still looking after Kassia, Luvic shrugged helplessly. Seron nodded, though he still looked sceptical. Taking these varied reactions for consent, Tremas took the Doctor aside, and they began talking in low voices.

Two armed Fosters patrolling the grounds around the Sanctum came into the courtyard outside the anteroom. They were astonished to see the giant form of Melkur stalking towards them.

As they fumbled for their weapons, twin beams lanced from Melkur's eyes. The two Fosters fell dead at its feet.

Melkur strode past them disappearing in the direction of the Grove.

*

The Doctor was studying the readings on Tremas's instrument. 'You took these readings in the Grove?'

Tremas nodded.

'Plasma fields of this strength couldn't have been generated without some pretty formidable magnetic containment,' said the Doctor thoughtfully. He began patting his pockets. 'I'm hardly tooled up for that kind of thing.'

Seron came over to them. 'Well, Tremas, what do you make of him? Does he talk sense?'

Tremas became aware that Kassia was staring at him with an almost hypnotic intensity. 'Yes, I think so,' he said hesitantly. 'It's hard to say.'

Kassia rose to her feet, suddenly filled with nervous energy once more. 'I say the strangers are a danger to us all and must be executed. Let us proceed.' Imperiously she beckoned the Fosters forward.

Tremas looked sadly at her. He hated to oppose her, especially when she was in this nervous state. But there was something unbalanced, obsessive, in her demands for the strangers' deaths, and he felt that his duty was clear. 'Wait! In honour to truth and justice, we cannot proceed. The charges against the strangers have not been proved.' Raising his voice, Tremas said formally, 'Consuls, under our sacred law, I claim Consular Privilege. I take these strangers under my protection.'

'No, Tremas,' cried Kassia passionately. She came close to him and clutched his arm. 'Can't you see? I am doing this for you.'

The other three Consuls looked on in astonishment. 'Consular Privilege,' mused Katura. 'It has not been called upon for generations.'

'That may be,' said Seron. 'Nevertheless, Consul Tremas is within his rights.'

Luvic sighed. 'Maybe he is. But I wish he'd tell us

39

what's going on.'

Katura turned to Tremas. 'Why this extraordinary gesture?'

'Yes, why?' demanded Kassia. 'Let it be! Let the strangers die.'

'Consular Privilege is Consular Privilege,' said Seron. 'We have no right to question Consul Tremas further.' He went over to the Doctor and Adric, and raised his hand. 'We hereby place you under the protection of Consul Tremas.'

Seron looked sharply at his colleague. 'Consul Tremas, you realise and accept the possible consequences?'

Tremas nodded.

'Consequences?' demanded the Doctor. 'What consequences?'

'Should it transpire that you are guilty after all, or should you infringe the laws here in any way, then the life of Consul Tremas will be forfeit with your own.'

'I see! Thank you, Consul Tremas, this is very civil of you. We'll do our best to deserve the compliment, won't we, Adric?'

Adric made no reply.

The Doctor jabbed him with a bony elbow. 'What? Oh, yes, we most certainly will.'

Tremas turned to see how Kassia was taking all this. To his astonishment, she was gone. 'Kassia? Where's Kassia?'

Adric pointed to the main door. 'She just went out through there.'

'Best let her go,' said Katura soothingly. 'It's just her way. Don't upset yourself.'

Tremas stared worriedly at the doorway, wondering where Kassia had gone, and what was happening to her.

Kassia ran down the steps from the Sanctum and stopped, appalled at the sight of the two crumpled bodies. 'No, Melkur, they must not be discovered. It is too soon.'

With the strength of one possessed, she seized the nearest body and dragged it across the courtyard and through the gate that led into the Grove. There she concealed it in thick foliage. She returned for the second body, the one nearest the door, and was just beginning to drag it away when she heard voices. To her horror, the door to the Sanctum began to open.

The door swung back and Katura and Luvic emerged. 'I hope the visitors are quite clear as to the terms of their bond to Consul Tremas.' Katura was saying.

'Yes indeed,' agreed Luvic fussily. 'It could be a very serious matter for them all.'

'But do they understand?' said old Katura peevishly. 'One never knows with strangers!'

At the foot of the steps, Seron paused, and turned to the Doctor and Adric. 'You both realise that you are now in the custody of Consul Tremas?'

'Yes indeed,' said the Doctor cheerfully.

'And that you must stay with him at all times?'

The Doctor said, 'Sort of house arrest, eh? Suits us quite well, doesn't it, Adric?'

'Suits you?' said Luvic, baffled.

Adric grinned. 'Well, with the TARDIS vanished we've nowhere to put up for the night.'

Tremas looked up at the sky, where the first pale streaks of light were appearing. 'There's little of the night left, Doctor. It will soon be dawn.'

'I will take my leave,' said Seron. 'Good night, Tremas.' He nodded stiffly to the others and strode away.

Katura and Luvic said their good-nights and followed him.

As soon as they were gone the Doctor knelt and felt the stone of the steps. 'It's been here!'

Adric looked round apprehensively. 'What has, Doctor?'

'Whatever it was,' said the Doctor mysteriously.

'How do you know?'

The Doctor held out his hand. It was dusted with a fine white powder. 'These stones have been hit by a plasma beam. The surface has disintegrated ...' They all looked down at the ground. Suddenly the Doctor pointed upwards. 'Look!'

Adric and Tremas looked up, startled.

'The sun's coming up! You're right, Tremas, it's morning already. You know what we need now, more than anything else?'

'What, Doctor?'

'Breakfast,' said the Doctor earnestly. 'Is your place far from here?'

Tremas smiled and led them away. As soon as they were out of sight, the Sanctum door swung closed again. Behind it was Kassia, the rapidly stiffening body of the second Foster in her arms. With feverish haste, she began dragging it towards the Grove.

Later that same morning, the Grove was calm and peaceful in the sunlight as a slender brown-haired girl in a flowing gauzy dress appeared, carrying a bunch of flowers. This was Nyssa, the daughter of Tremas's first marriage.

She knelt and placed the flowers at the foot of Melkur. The statue stood in its usual place, gazing impassively across the Grove.

Standing, Nyssa peered up at the towering figure, seeming to stare intently into its face.

From inside the patch of shrubbery Kassia crouched watching her. 'No,' whispered Kassia. 'No!'

Nyssa reached up and brushed away a leaf that was clinging to Melkur's face. She stepped back, surveyed the statue for a moment, then turned and left the Grove.

When she was gone, Kassia emerged from her hiding place and stood before Melkur.

The silky voice that seemed to reverberate inside her mind said, 'Ah, Kassia!'

Trembling, Kassia said, 'Yes, Melkur?'

Tremas's quarters were an interesting mixture of classical furnishings and scientific equipment. Here, the Doctor, Adric and Tremas were finishing a simple but satisfying breakfast—wholemeal bread, assorted fruits and cheeses, and a fruit-juice cordial. Tremas plied them hospitably with food, though he himself ate sparingly—he was worried about Kassia, who had not returned to her sleeping quarters and was presumably wandering somewhere in the gardens. The Doctor, however, had a hearty breakfast, and since Adric usually ate enough for two the food was soon polished off.

The Doctor pushed his plate aside. 'Well, it's high time we got to work!'

Tremas looked curiously at him. 'What do you have in mind, Doctor?'

'I'd feel a lot happier if I could find out what's

happened to the TARDIS. It's got to be there somewhere.'

'Your space-craft? Proctor Neman had the Grove most thoroughly searched and—' He broke off as a slender dark-haired girl came in.

'Father, I—' She stopped abruptly at the sight of the two visitors.

'My daughter, Nyssa,' said Tremas. 'Nyssa, this is the Doctor, and this is Adric. They will be our guests for a while.'

'I've heard all about you two,' said Nyssa. 'How do you feel?'

'Fine, fine,' said the Doctor. 'It always cheers me up to be reprieved.'

Nyssa looked curiously at Adric. 'Hello!'

'Hello,' said Adric rather indistinctly. He was just finishing the last piece of cheese.

'What were you saying about searching the Grove?' asked Nyssa. 'I've just come from there.'

The Doctor looked hopefully at her. 'You didn't happen to notice a sort of blue box thing with a lamp on top, did you?'

'There was nothing like that there.'

The Doctor jumped to his feet. 'Well, it's there somewhere. Maybe the chameleon circuit's suddenly started working. We'd better go and take a look.'

Tremas rose. 'Very well, Doctor, I can take you to the Grove, but only you. Adric must stay here. Nyssa, you will entertain our guest.'

Kassia stared fearfully up at the blank face of the statue. 'I tried to have the Doctor destroyed, Melkur, but Tremas intervened and so I failed. The Doctor is now protected by our sacred law.'

The silken voice said, 'Your failure is unimportant. The law which protects the Doctor will presently destroy him.'

'What of Tremas, my husband? You promised to save him for me. He must not become Keeper.'

There was a sinister chuckle. 'Your precious Keepers are irrelevant now. When this one dies, he will be the last of his kind.'

'But Tremas is already Keeper-Nominate.'

'Perhaps.' There was a sardonic amusement in the voice. 'But what's in a name? Kassia is as good a name as Tremas.'

'I do not understand, Melkur.'

'Understanding is not necessary to your task, Kassia. You need only listen carefully—and obey!'

5

Melkur's Secret

Although they were a little wary of each other at first, Adric and Nyssa were soon well on the way to becoming friends. Adric was cheerful and easy-going by nature, and Nyssa was a pleasant, friendly girl, starved for company of her own age. Tremas was the only one of the Consuls to have children. Since his duties meant he had to live close to the Sanctum, Nyssa spent much of her time with older people.

As for Adric, he was beginning to feel that, from the Keeper downwards, practically everyone on Traken was old, eminent, and bearded.

Nyssa had inherited her father's interest in science, and soon she was showing Adric Tremas's work-bench.

Adric picked up Tremas's energy-scanner. 'This is pretty impressive.'

'My father built it himself,' said Nyssa proudly.

'I had no idea your technology was so advanced.'

'Most of the other Consuls refuse to bother with science,' said Nyssa scornfully. 'They just rely on the Keeper and on the Source. But it is our duty to protect and expand the great power which the Keeper exercises on our behalf.' She spoke the words as if she'd learned them by heart, and it was obvious she was quoting Tremas.

'The Doctor told me about your Keeper. I gather the

chosen Keeper dedicates himself totally to this bioelectronic system.'

'The Source,' said Nyssa proudly. 'Through it the Keeper organises all the resources of the Traken Union. You might almost say he becomes the Source.'

Adric was studying the readings on the energy-scanner. 'These readings are tremendously high. I don't suppose this thing could be picking up the Source itself?'

Nyssa shook her head. 'The frequency profiles of the energy emissions are something completely new to us.'

'Have you tried a Fourier analysis?' said Adric suddenly.

Nyssa shook her head.

'Have you got something to write on?'

She passed him a plastic notepad and a pen, and Adric began scribbling calculations at furious speed. After a few minutes he looked up. 'Nyssa.'

'What is it?'

I think I might just be able to work out what's causing these energy emissions!'

Unlike those of Tremas, Seron's quarters were furnished in classic Traken style, with none of the scientific clutter that characterised Tremas's home.

Seron was looking in outraged astonishment at a delegation of his fellow Consuls, Katura, Luvic and Kassia. They had visited him soon after breakfast. 'What is this?' demanded Seron peevishly. 'Secret meetings now, is it? Why do you visit my quarters all hugger-mugger like this?'

Katura said, 'Kassia tells us that her husband has been concealing vital knowledge from the Consuls. Is this true, Seron?'

'What knowledge?'

'Knowledge concerning the true nature of these mysterious energy emissions. Tremas has been recording their energy profiles.'

'Nothing is worse than disharmony and distrust between Consuls,' said Seron wearily. 'Tremas did not conceal his knowledge. He discussed the subject fully—with me!'

Luvic was shocked. 'Then you knew as well! You shared in the concealment. This is a grave matter, Seron.'

'Tremas was in possession of dangerous, disturbing knowledge,' said Seron impatiently. 'I advised him to keep it to himself.'

Katura was outraged. 'Why? By what right?'

'If knowledge of Tremas's discoveries were to spread, it might easily tip our people over the brink into a chaos of superstition. Is that what you want, Consuls?'

'This matter has grave implications for the succession,' said Kassia.

Seron looked at her in astonishment. 'You question the wisdom of the Keeper's choice? You imply that Tremas is unfit to succeed him?'

'There is only one way that this matter can be resolved. Tremas must prove his fitness—and the sooner the better. He must enter Rapport.'

'Rapport?' said Seron unbelievingly. 'Rapport with the Keeper?'

A Consul whose ideas or policies were in dispute, whose conduct was in any way suspect could chose to undergo Rapport. His mind was linked directly to that of the Keeper. If his integrity was lacking or his purposes impure, the energy of the Source would surely kill him. If he survived, he was vindicated, with all the authority of the Keeper behind him.

Seron looked wonderingly at Kassia. 'You would ask your husband to risk his life?'

Kassia returned his gaze unflinchingly. 'It is the only way that this matter can be resolved. What is there to fear, Seron? If Tremas acted justly, he will survive, and we will be humbled.'

Seron could be over-anxious and officious, a stickler for rules and regulations and the letter of the law. But he was a man of the highest integrity, and his dedication to the service of Traken was absolute. 'Tremas did what he did on my advice. If there is error or deceit, then I am to blame.'

Katura stared at him. 'You, Seron?' The thought of Seron being in error was almost inconceivable.

'Then in that case,' said Luvic slowly, 'you are the one who should enter Rapport.'

'That is my intention.'

'No!' burst out Kassia. 'That is not what was intended.'

'Intended, Kassia?' said Seron sharply. 'By whom?'

Kassia did not reply.

'Very well. Now that this question has been raised, let us put it to the rest. I shall submit myself to Rapport. I ask that Consul Tremas keep vigil on my behalf.'

'Consul Tremas is also under suspicion,' said Katura. 'He is hardly the best choice.'

'I shall keep vigil for you, Consul Seron,' said Kassia.

Seron nodded coldly. 'Very well, Consul Kassia. Under your vigilant eye we may be certain that justice will be done. And now I must prepare myself. If you will excuse me?' Responding to the hint, the Consuls took their leave.

*

When the Doctor and Tremas reached the gate that led to the Grove, they found it guarded by armed Fosters, under the command of Proctor Neman. A sizeable crowd had gathered around the gate, and the Fosters were having considerable difficulty in keeping them out of the Grove itself.

The Doctor and Tremas halted a little way off. 'What's going on?' asked the Doctor.

Tremas beckoned Proctor Neman forward. When Neman came up to them, Tremas said, 'We intend to visit the Grove, Proctor Neman. Who are all these people?'

'Ordinary citizens, Consul.'

'What are they doing here?'

'Waiting for a sign from Melkur.'

'A sign?'

'There is a rumour that Melkur has been redeemed, and will bring the recent disasters to an end.'

'Hardly seems likely, does it?' said the Doctor.

'Superstitious nonsense,' said Neman, a little uneasily. 'But if I may make a suggestion, Consul?'

'Yes, Proctor Neman?'

'It might be better if you did not visit the Grove, just at present. It might be taken as some kind of confirmation of the rumours. We're having enough trouble controlling them as it is.'

'I can see the problem,' said the Doctor. 'But all the same—' He broke off, catching a tiny shake of the head from Tremas.

'Very well,' said Tremas briskly. 'I'll show the Doctor around the Court and the gardens instead. Come along, Doctor!'

As they moved away, Tremas said in a low voice, 'There is another way into the Grove. Through the service vault beneath the Keeper's Chamber.'

50

'Won't we find worried citizens hanging about there too?'

'No. The passage is secret. Besides, entry is only possible by use of the consular rings.' Holding up his hand, Tremas showed the ring he had used in summoning the Keeper. 'Come, Doctor.'

They hurried away.

Adric checked over his calculations for the last time. He looked up at Nyssa. 'You're sure these readings were taken before we arrived.'

'I'm positive. Do you know what caused them?'

'I've got a pretty good idea—except that it's impossible. The Doctor will know for sure, though. I must show him these notes right away.'

Thrusting the notes inside his tunic, Adric headed for the door.

'But you're supposed to stay with me,' protested Nyssa.

'Then you'd better come too,' said Adric logically. 'Come on, we're going to the Grove.'

Once more Kassia stood before Melkur, the twin beams from his eyes playing on her face.

'You have served me well, Kassia. At my feet you will find a gift. Wear it as a token of your allegiance to me.'

Kassia looked down and saw a plain silver collar at the base of the statue. She picked it up, opened it, and put it round her neck. As the collar closed it seemed to fuse and tighten. Kassia tugged at the fastening, and found it was impossible to open it.

'Now your allegiance is assured,' whispered Melkur. 'Go now Kassia, and be my eyes and ears.'

'I do not understand, Melkur,' said Kassia worriedly. 'It has not happened as you planned. Seron, not Tremas will enter Rapport.'

'There is much that you do not understand, Kassia.'

There were two huge screens above the console in the control room. They looked strangely like eyes. Both screens showed Kassia, staring imploringly upwards. A speaker relayed her anxious voice.

'I know that I have failed you, Melkur. But spare my husband, I beg of you. Remember your promise.'

Again there came that soft, eerie chuckle. A withered hand reached out and touched a control, and the eye-screens went dead.

Like the Doctor and Tremas, Adric and Nyssa stopped in astonishment at the sight of the crowd around the gate that led into the Grove.

Adric was about to go on, but Nyssa held him back. 'It's no good, we'll never get in with all these people.'

'I thought you were allowed to go in.'

'I am. The Keeper appointed me to tend Melkur. But since there's been all this trouble the Fosters are guarding the gate. They'd never let me take you in.'

'Is there any other way into the Grove?'

'Yes. I imagine the Doctor and father are using it.'

'Then what are we waiting for?'

'It's no use, Adric. We can only use the secret way if my father or some other Consul is with us. It needs a consular ring to open it—and I doubt if any of the other Consuls will help us.'

'Then we'll have to get in this way,' said Adric obstinately.

52

Nyssa thought hard for a moment, looking at the sturdy form of Proctor Neman. 'There might be a way. I'll have to go back and fetch something first, though.'

'Fetch what? Some kind of weapon?'

Nyssa smiled. 'You might say that. A weapon that opens most doors—even on Traken. You wait here.'

The massive doors to the Inner Sanctum were closed. Set into them was an almost invisible slot. Tremas inserted the stone of his ring, and the door slid silently open. The Doctor and Tremas went through, and the door closed behind them.

The Inner Sanctum was silent and empty. Tremas led the way to the Keeper's dome. Above the empty throne the Source flame burned bright and clear. Tremas walked round to a door set in the wall. He was about to open it when suddenly a small light began blinking above the door.

'Someone's in there,' whispered Tremas. 'You'd better not be seen, Doctor.'

They retreated behind the shelter of a pillar.

After a moment the door opened and Kassia emerged. Staring blankly ahead of her, she glided across the Sanctum as if sleepwalking.

Tremas moved to follow her, but the Doctor pulled him back. 'Best leave her alone. She appears to be in some kind of hypnotic trance.'

They watched unseen as Kassia walked to the Sanctum doors, opened them with her consular ring, and went outside.

Tremas looked worriedly after her for a moment, and then went over to the door from which she had emerged. He touched a control, and the door slid open.

Tremas waved the Doctor through, and then followed him inside.

The Doctor found himself in a stone passage which led down some steps, through an arch, and into a brightly lit chamber. Storage racks lined the wall, loaded with a variety of bioelectronic equipment. Set into the far wall was an enormous globe, glowing and pulsing with energy. Beneath it was a complex control panel.

The Doctor headed straight for the globe, looking at it in fascination.

'This is the Source Manipulator,' said Tremas proudly. 'Its functions have expanded steadily over the years.'

Admiringly the Doctor studied the globe and its control panel. 'Limitless organising capacity, refined to a single flame, obedient only to the will of your Keeper! A great achievement, Tremas—and a great temptation, to others less principled than ourselves.'

'The thought had occurred to me,' said Tremas ruefully. 'Come, Doctor, the Grove is this way.'

He led the Doctor through the door at the far end of the storage chamber, along another, narrower passage ending in a door. Tremas opened the door to reveal a dark opening overhung with trailing vines.

They went through the door and emerged into the Grove.

In the twin-screened control room, a warning bleep sounded. The hooded figure hunched over the console reached out for a control, and the screens sprang to life. They showed the Doctor and Tremas, both staring upwards.

The watcher heard the Doctor's voice say, 'So this is

Melkur! Makes you uneasy, doesn't he, Tremas?'

'Yes,' said Tremas grimly. 'And with good reason.'

The Doctor gave the great statue a last curious glance and then turned away. 'I want to take a good look at him later on. But first, the TARDIS.' He took a few paces forward. 'I set her down just about—here!'

The Doctor fished a small circular device from his pocket and waved it gently to and fro. It emitted a low, musical hum, which suddenly rose in pitch. 'I knew it,' said the Doctor triumphantly. 'It's here all right. Just been displaced slightly from the current time frame.'

Tremas stared blankly at him.

'It's just a few seconds ahead of us,' explained the Doctor. 'So whenever we're here, it's just gone!' He put the time-scanner away and rubbed his chin. 'Now what's the simplest way around this?' He looked hopefully at Tremas. 'I want to set up a standing wave, something the auto-systems can home in on.'

To his relief, Tremas found he could understand the theory, if not the application. 'Would a binary inductive system serve your purpose, Doctor?'

'It would be an excellent starting point.'

'Good. We must return to the storage vault.'

As they moved away, the twin screens showed their receding forms. The cloaked and hooded figure in the control room chuckled hoarsely. 'Find your TARDIS if you can, Time Lord. Much good will it do you. It is too late to save you now!'

6

The Net

When Nyssa returned to the gate of the Grove, she was carrying a heavy purse.

Adric looked at her impatiently. 'Where's this weapon of yours then?'

'Here,' said Nyssa and hefted the purse.

Adric heard the faint click of coins. 'Ah, I see!'

Nyssa went closer to the group of Fosters by the gate, and Adric followed.

Close to the gate, Nyssa paused and beckoned imperiously. 'Proctor Neman!'

Neman came over to them and saluted. 'Yes, my lady?'

'Proctor Neman, why are these people gathered here?'

Neman told her of the rumours about Melkur. 'Superstitious nonsense, my lady—but they are breaking no law.'

'They offend the dignity of the Keeper,' said Nyssa loftily. 'Have them removed.'

'It is not lawful for me to send them away, lady.'

Nyssa hefted the purse in her hand. 'My father and his fellow Consuls determine what is lawful.'

Neman hesitated, eyeing the purse and then turned to his men. 'Remove them!'

The Fosters began driving the citizens away. They were grumbling and sullen, and slow to move at first, but the citizens of Traken were a law-abiding group with no tradition of rebellion, and gradually the crowd ebbed away.

Proctor Neman himself, however, showed no signs of moving. 'It is done, my lady.'

Nyssa tossed him the purse. 'Go with them, make sure that they are cleared from the area.'

Tucking the purse inside his tunic, Neman saluted and followed his men.

As he disappeared around the corner, Nyssa turned to Adric. 'Hurry!'

They hurried over to the gate. Nyssa shoved at it, but it refused to budge. 'It's locked.'

'Never mind,' said Adric cheerfully. 'I'm quite good with locks.' He pointed to the brooch on the shoulder of Nyssa's dress. 'May I?'

She unfastened the brooch and passed it to him, and Adric inserted the long pin into the lock, feeling for the tumblers. A few minutes later the lock clicked open.

Adric heaved at the gate, but it was stiff and heavy, difficult to move. Nyssa came to help him, and they managed to open it far enough for Adric to slip through. 'Come on, Nyssa!'

Nyssa was just about to follow when Consuls Katura and Luvic appeared round the corner, followed by Proctor Neman and his Fosters.

At the sight of Nyssa standing by the gate Katura called, 'No, Nyssa. Do not enter the Grove!'

Helplessly, Nyssa waited until they came up to her.

'The Grove is dangerous at the present time,' said Luvic.

'Who says so?'

'Your father,' said Katura firmly. 'Consul Seron, too.'

At a nod from Luvic, Proctor Neman pulled the

57

massive gate closed again, and the lock clicked home.

Katura patted Nyssa on the shoulder. 'I'm sure Melkur can do without your attention for one day.'

'Unfortunately the State cannot do without ours,' said Luvic ruefully, 'and your father has disappeared somewhere.'

Katura nodded. 'There are grave matters to be decided Nyssa. I think you had better go home now. The Fosters will escort you.'

Before she could protest, Nyssa was led away.

Flattened against the wall on the other side of the gate, Adric realised he was on his own. He moved cautiously into the Grove.

The little group of Consuls and Fosters headed for Seron's quarters. They found him waiting for them, dressed in his ceremonial robes, his face pale but calm.

'It is time Consul Seron,' said Katura.

Seron surveyed them impassively. 'Very well, Consul Katura. Let us proceed to the Sanctum.'

Adric edged his way through the dense shrubbery, brushing low branches and trailing creepers from his face. Even in the morning sunlight there was something very sinister about the Grove.

Adric looked round uneasily. 'I'm not going to let a few old weeds frighten me. Anyway, the Doctor must be here—somewhere.'

He came out into the clearing where they had left the now-vanished TARDIS. The giant form of Melkur seemed to glare down at him. Adric stared up at the terrifying stone face in fascination.

*

As Adric's worried face looked up into the twin eye-screens, the hooded figure chuckled evilly. 'So, Doctor, your sheep stray from the fold!' It reached for a control, and a light on the console glowed red.

Adric frowned. Was it his imagination, or were the slitted eyes starting to glow?

A hand came down on his shoulder and he spun round in astonishment.

The hooded figure touched another control, and the light on the console faded.

With a gasp of relief, Adric saw the Doctor and Tremas behind him.

'Thought I heard you crashing about,' said the Doctor severely. 'I told you to stay with Nyssa.'

'But I've found out something, Doctor. At least, I think I have. I've got to talk to you.'

'Can't it wait?'

'No!'

'All right. This way. We're down here.'

The Doctor and Tremas led Adric back to the secret door.

Moving in a solemn procession, the little group came to a halt outside the door to the Inner Sanctum.

Katura looked at Seron. 'You are ready?'

'I am ready.'

'So be it. We wish you good fortune.'

Seron held out his hand, and Katura removed his

consular ring from his finger.

She inserted the stone of her own ring into the locking device and the door slid open.

Seron entered the Sanctum, followed by Kassia, and the door closed behind them.

Seron was about to enter Rapport.

In the storage vault, Adric waited anxiously while the Doctor studied his calculations. He looked around the room, taking in the endless racks of bioelectronic supplies. On a work-bench nearby some kind of complicated electronic apparatus was in the process of being assembled—one of the Doctor's typical lash-ups, thought Adric.

The Doctor put down Adric's notes and frowned.

'Well, Doctor?' asked Adric anxiously. 'I'm right, surely. That particular wave-loop pattern is unmistakable.'

Tremas gave him a look of mild astonishment. 'Do I take it you believe you have identified the source of the energy emissions?'

'I think they might be from some kind of TARDIS,' said Adric simply. 'I don't know what the Doctor thinks.'

The Doctor patted Adric on the shoulder. 'The Doctor thinks you might very well be right. This is certainly caused by something very like a TARDIS generator, though you don't get shift ratios of this kind from a humble Type Forty like mine.' The Doctor turned back to the work-benches. 'And speaking of the TARDIS, it's time we got on with getting ours back. Adric, we have a fold-back flow inducer in the making here. Your assistance, please!' They set to work.

*

Head bowed, Seron stood just before the Chamber of the Keeper, Kassia a pace or two behind him.

'Keeper of Traken,' said Seron in a low, vibrant voice. 'The integrity of your Consul has been challenged. I therefore claim Rapport with the Source, so that you may make your judgement.'

Kassia moved to the controls at the base of the Chamber. The flame above the empty throne blazed higher.

The Doctor stepped back from the bench. 'There we are,' he said proudly, 'a fully fledged, portable, fold-back flow inducer!'

To Adric it looked like a power-pack, a set of switches and a random assortment of electronic spares, all bolted together in a fairly haphazard fashion, but no doubt the Doctor knew what he was talking about.

Suddenly Tremas pointed towards the Source Manipulator. Strange cloudy forms were swirling about inside it. 'Look, Doctor, there is activity in the Source. The Keeper is being summoned!'

The flame was burning brightly now, casting a golden radiance over Seron's face. Suddenly a glowing beam of light shot out from the Chamber and enfolded him. Seron stiffened and flung his head back, his whole form tense with agony. He staggered and almost fell.

The light faded and there in the Chamber sat the wizened form of the Keeper. He looked incredibly old, infinitely weary and sad.

Seron drew a deep, sobbing breath. 'Your judgement, Keeper?'

In a feeble, almost inaudible voice the Keeper

61

whispered, 'You are guiltless, Seron ... but you are doomed! We are both betrayed!'

The Keeper pointed a trembling finger at Kassia. The silver collar around her neck was beginning to glow with a faint eerie radiance, as the Keeper, quite suddenly, faded away.

Eyes wide, Kassia stared hypnotically at Seron. 'Forgive me, Seron. I serve a greater purpose.'

Seron drew himself upright. 'Lost, degraded creature ...'

Kassia's eyes began to glow redly.

Seron faced her, unafraid. 'You have betrayed your Keeper and your most sacred Consular vows. Reject this evil, Kassia. Reject it!

'I cannot,' gasped Kassia. 'Now, Melkur, now!'

Her anguished face stared into the twin eye-screens. The hooded figure leaned forward and jabbed a control.

Twin beams of energy lanced from Kassia's eyes, striking Seron full in the face. Seron pitched forward and fell.

The Doctor, Tremas and Adric stood listening at the other side of the door that led from the storage vaults into the Sanctum.

'I hear nothing,' said Tremas worriedly.

The Doctor nodded towards the door, and Tremas opened it. They came out into the Sanctum—and found Kassia staring down at the body of Seron.

She looked up guiltily as Tremas appeared.

Tremas went to kneel by the body, then looked up at Kassia. 'He is dead,' he said unbelievingly. 'What have you done, Kassia?'

He rose and went towards her. She backed away,

62

clutching at the silver band around her neck. 'Tremas ... my husband! I did it for you!'

The main door of the Sanctum opened, admitting Katura and Luvic, followed by two Fosters.

They stopped on the threshold, staring appalled at Seron's body.

Kassia drew herself upright, and spoke in a fierce, strained voice that did not seem to be her own. 'Consuls! Seron is dead, rejected by the Keeper. The Keeper says he was an agent of Melkur—as are these three here! In a sweeping gesture she indicated the Doctor, Adric, and her husband, Tremas.

Luvic appeared stunned. 'First Seron, and now you, Tremas. Nothing is sacred any more, it seems.'

'Take them, Fosters!' ordered Kassia.

As the armed Fosters moved forward, the Doctor yelled, 'Adric, Tremas—the vault!'

The Fosters sprang forward, but they were still only on the threshold of the Sanctum. Before the Fosters could reach the still-open door, the three fugitives had dashed through it, closed it behind them, and locked it from the other side.

The Fosters began hammering at the door. Kassia shouted. 'No, leave it! Come with me!'

The Doctor, Adric and Tremas dashed down the passage and through the storage vault, the Doctor pausing on the way to snatch up the fold-back flow inducer.

'Hurry, Doctor,' called Tremas.

'What's the use?' gasped Adric. 'The Fosters will be heading for the Grove by now!'

'You're forgetting the TARDIS, Adric. If we can get it back and get inside it in time ...'

They ran for the stairs.

Soon they were pushing their way through the

overgrown shrubbery, to the spot where they had last seen the TARDIS. The Doctor set up the apparatus just in front of the statue of Melkur, and switched it on. Immediately it began emitting a rhythmic, high-pitched electronic whine.

Adric looked dubiously down at the strange-looking apparatus. 'Do you really think it'll work, Doctor?'

'Well, give it a minute or two,' said the Doctor irritably. 'Just trust me. Or alternatively, if you come up with a better idea—let me know!'

A deep, sibilant voice whispered, 'Doctor!'

They all swung round. The eyes of the giant statue were glowing red. 'Very ingenious, Doctor. But recovering the TARDIS will not help you now.'

The Doctor stared curiously at the statue. There was something strangely familiar about that voice. 'Melkur! So you are the cause of all this!'

'Turn off your primitive instrument, Doctor!' commanded the voice.

Tremas was gazing up at the statue in horrified astonishment, and suddenly twin light beams sprang from its eyes.

'Look out,' yelled the Doctor. 'Don't look in its eyes!'

Tremas flung his arm across his eyes and staggered back. His foot turned on a loose stone and he crashed to the ground.

'Doctor, look!' called Adric.

The Doctor turned and saw the familiar blue shape of the TARDIS materialising before him. 'It worked!' he yelled. He grabbed the fallen Tremas and began dragging him towards the TARDIS.

Kassia came running through the Grove, armed Fosters at her heels. She sprang in front of the TARDIS, barring their escape.

Tremas struggled painfully to his feet. 'Help us, Kassia!'

Kassia stared fixedly at him, her words echoing his own. 'Help me, Tremas. Help me!'

She reached out her hands to him, but the silver collar glowed and tightened, and she clutched at her throat.

Tremas took her by the shoulders, gazing agonisedly into her face.

For a moment the personality of the Kassia he knew and loved seemed to re-assert itself.

'Don't look,' she gasped. 'Don't look into my eyes!' With a convulsive effort she jerked her head aside so that the twin beams from her eyes merely brushed Tremas's face. He staggered back, falling to the ground once more.

The Doctor sprang to his side. 'Help me, Adric. He's only stunned.'

With a last desperate effort they dragged Tremas almost to the TARDIS door. Suddenly a net descended on them, trapping all three in its folds.

Adric looked and saw that the net had apparently been fired from some device held by one of the Fosters.

The Foster touched a control, a fierce shock jolted through Adric's body, and he knew no more.

Kassia's face was as blank and as calm as the statue itself. 'It is done, Melkur.'

Melkur's voice said, 'Oh, no, Kassia. It is just beginning!'

7

Prisoners of Melkur

The cell was in the form of a long cellar, with an arched stone roof, a heavy metal grille barring the far end, and bunks along the walls. The Fosters opened the grille dumped the semi-conscious bodies of the Doctor, Adric and Tremas on the bunks, then left, slamming the grille shut, and locking it behind them.

Kassia and Neman watched the process from the corridor outside the cell. When the process was complete, Kassia said, 'They must be closely guarded at all times. They are to have no contact with anyone without my authority.'

'Yes, Consul.' Neman hesitated. 'What is to become of them?'

'My husband and his friends have betrayed the Keeper,' said Kassia coldly. 'I shall require a full confession to satisfy the Traken people and then . . . You understand me?'

'Yes, Consul.'

'Excellent. Your services will not be overlooked, Proctor Neman.' Kassia strode away.

Outside the Sanctum she found Katura and Luvic, their heads together in serious discussion.

'Ah, Kassia,' said Luvic, with an attempt at his usual cheerfulness. 'Where are the strangers?'

'Closely guarded.'

'And—Tremas?'

'Consul Tremas is with them.' Kassia looked hard at the two remaining Consuls, dominating them with the force of her personality. 'It is our duty to the Keeper to propose a new successor. Tremas has forfeited his right, and Seron is dead.'

'It must be one of us three, then,' said Luvic.

Katura nodded. 'We must come to our formal decision at the proper time.'

Kassia nodded, coldly, and walked away.

Groaning and rubbing their aching limbs, the three prisoners were taking stock of their situation.

The Doctor looked round. 'Quite a little home from home, isn't it?'

'We are in the old penal wing, Doctor,' said Tremas. 'We have had no use for cells like this for many years.'

'Not till we came along, eh?' The Doctor went over to the grille and peered through it, examining the area of the lock.

'Can you get us out of here, Doctor?' asked Adric.

'A rather old-fashioned electron lock, I think. The sonic screwdriver should deal with it easily enough.' But the Doctor didn't move.

'Get on with it, then,' said Adric.

'Unfortunately the control panel is well out of reach.' The Doctor fished the sonic screwdriver from his pocket. 'Be a good chap—nip outside and open it for me.'

Adric groaned. 'Is that all you can do?'

'I'm not a magician, you know,' said the Doctor plaintively.

They heard footsteps in the corridor, and soon two patrolling Fosters marched by.

'Lovely day,' called the Doctor.

The Fosters ignored him.

Kassia stood in the Grove, looking up at Melkur, the twin rays from the statue's glowing eyes illuminating her face. 'All is as you predicted, Melkur. Seron is dead, Tremas in disgrace. He cannot become Keeper now. You have saved him.'

'Tremas will continue to live,' whispered Melkur. 'As long as you continue to obey.'

'Is there yet more to be done?'

'Oh yes, my servant. Much more. The Doctor is a most cunning enemy. While he still lives, the cause of Melkur is in danger.'

'Must the boy die also?'

'Yes! The Doctor and his young friend . . . You must finish what you have begun, Kassia. When they are both dead, your husband can be pardoned and restored to you.'

Kassia bowed her head. 'My thanks, Melkur.'

'One other thing. You have interfered with the succession. Now order must be restored.'

'I have spoken with the Consuls. A successor is to be chosen.'

'And will this successor serve me as you do, Kassia?'

'I do not know, Melkur.'

'But we must know, Kassia,' said the soft voice. 'These things must be ensured. I can think of no better Keeper than yourself.'

At last Kassia saw the trap into which she had fallen.

'No, Melkur, no! You promised you would release me!'

She heard Melkur's mocking laughter. 'Not until the work is done, Kassia!'

*

The Doctor sat on his bunk, chin in hands. 'At least the Keeper isn't dead yet. We still have a little time.'

'Only a very little,' said Tremas. 'The Keeper was unable to prevent the murder of Seron. His power must be almost at an end. His death cannot be far off now.'

'Whatever happens, Melkur must not take control of the Source.'

'How could he, Doctor? The bioelectronic structure will only permit a native of Traken to succeed to the office of Keeper.'

'Exactly!'

Tremas stared at him in horror. 'Kassia?'

The Doctor nodded. 'Kassia.'

After waiting for what seemed hours for the Doctor, Tremas and Adric to return, Nyssa determined to go and look for them. To provide a reason for her visit to the Grove, she gathered a bunch of flowers. She told the Foster on the gate that she was visiting Melkur, in accordance with the instructions of the Keeper, and the man let her through.

As she approached the statue, Nyssa saw Kassia kneeling before it, tears streaming down her face.

She seemed to be talking to Melkur. 'Melkur, I implore you, answer me.'

Ducking into the undergrowth, Nyssa began to edge closer.

Kassia was still pleading with the statue. 'I beg you, Melkur, grant me my release.'

Nyssa moved closer—too close because Kassia heard her. Springing to her feet, Kassia caught hold of her. Nyssa struggled furiously, dropping her flowers, but Kassia was too strong for her, and soon Nyssa was dragged from her hiding place.

Kassia held her wrists in a cruel grip. 'Spying! My Fosters will deal with you!'

'Your Fosters?' said Nyssa angrily. 'The Fosters serve the Consuls, and the people of Traken.'

Kassia smiled coldly. 'They are my Fosters now, bought and paid for.'

'You haven't bought my father—or Adric and the Doctor.'

'No need. All three are safely under lock and key.'

'My father is no criminal, Kassia, nor are the strangers. I think Melkur has made you mad.'

Suddenly Kassia's manner changed. Releasing the girl, she said gently, 'Do not interfere with things you cannot understand, Nyssa. Go home. This will all come to good in time. My husband, your father, will be restored to us.'

Nyssa stared at her for a moment, and then turned and fled.

Sobbing, Kassia fell to her knees amongst the trampled flowers.

Nyssa went straight home, but non-interference was the last thing on her mind. She went into Tremas's study and rooted about until she found an empty instrument case. Going to a wall-rack she took down a torch-like device, adjusted the controls in its base, put it in the case, and hurried away.

Kassia, Katura and Luvic sat at the conference table in the Inner Sanctum. With two Council members missing, the table looked curiously bare.

Kassia looked from one to the other of the two remaining Consuls. 'Consuls of Traken, recent events have shown that great evil threatens the Traken Union. It is our clear duty to unite in order to defeat that evil. Are we agreed?'

'Naturally, Kassia,' said old Katura sharply. 'We are all proud of our liberal traditions, but now we must act to defend them. This superstitious mania, this cult of Melkur seems to be growing steadily stronger.'

'I fear that it was fostered by my husband, and by the strangers.'

'It must be stopped,' said Luvic solemnly.

'And so it will be, Consuls,' said Kassia. 'But only if we demonstrate our determination to crush it. And to do so effectively we need a new Keeper-Nominate, one who will not shirk the task that must be done.'

'That is certainly true, Kassia,' said Katura wearily. 'But I am too old now, and as for Luvic ...'

Luvic sighed. 'I fear I do not have such greatness in me.'

They both looked at Kassia.

'You see,' said Katura gently. 'There is no great problem about the choice, Kassia.'

Nyssa found Proctor Neman checking the guard outside the Sanctum. 'I was looking for you, Neman.'

Neman looked curiously at the box in Nyssa's hands. 'How may I serve you, lady?'

'By letting me see my father.'

'I am sorry lady, but it isn't possible.'

'My father is still a Consul of Traken. I demand to see him.'

'Your father and the strangers are condemned as criminals. No one may see them.'

'By whose orders?'

'By the orders of Consul Kassia. Forgive me lady but

71

I have no choice.'

'Please, Proctor Neman,' pleaded Nyssa.

The meeting of the diminished Council was still in progress.

'So be it,' Katura was saying. 'Consul Kassia, we appoint you Keeper-Nominate. Do you accept this office.'

After a long pause Kassia said, 'I accept.'

'It is done then.'

'Now we must decide on the matter of the strangers,' said Luvic unhappily. 'And, if you will forgive me, on the fate of Tremas.'

'The strangers must die,' said Kassia instantly. 'Tremas may in time be pardoned. He can still be of use to us.'

'Yes indeed,' said Luvic. 'We must not forget to take his past record into account. His contribution to the welfare of the Union has been quite outstanding. Must the strangers die?'

Kassia said, 'The death of the strangers is necessary to deter other potential traitors.'

Katura said sadly. 'Yes. If only to show that our intentions are firm—they must be executed.'

Proctor Neman refused to listen to Nyssa's pleas. Finally she put her hand inside the box. 'I have something here that will help to change your mind.'

Neman smiled. 'I cannot accept payment from you, lady. The fate of the Traken Union is at stake. There is a limit to the power of money.'

Nyssa produced the torch-device and pointed it at him. 'I think this will be powerful enough to convince you.'

Neman looked mildly amused. 'I take it that is some kind of weapon, lady?'

'Open the cell door,' said Nyssa firmly. 'Please do as I ask. I will use it if I must.'

Neman saw that she was serious. 'You will die for this, lady.'

'I know what I am doing. Now, the keys to the cell, please.'

Neman shrugged. Reaching inside his tunic, he produced a case which held several thin metal strips, the coded keys for the electronic locks in the detention sector.

He held it out, but as Nyssa reached to take it Neman grabbed for the weapon in her hand.

Nyssa stepped back and fired. A green ray shot from the device and Neman fell, dropping the keys. The Foster tried to draw his weapon, but Nyssa shot him down before he could reach it. Looking rather appalled at what she had done, Nyssa snatched up the keys and fled.

The Doctor lay back on his bunk, hands behind his head. 'Not a very chatty lot, these Fosters of yours!'

'I imagine Kassia has bribed them well,' said Tremas. 'She dare not risk losing us now.'

'It's always nice to be wanted,' said the Doctor idly. He sat up at the sight of Nyssa peering through the grille. 'Ah, a friendly face at last!'

'Nyssa!' said Tremas in astonishment.

Nyssa put her finger to her lips, signalling him to be quiet.

The Doctor fished out his sonic screwdriver. 'Nyssa—you can open the lock with this!'

Nyssa shook her head, holding up the key-case.

'New technology dates so quickly these days,' said

73

the Doctor sadly. He put the sonic screwdriver away. Seconds later the grille swung back and they all hurried out into the corridor.

Tremas gave Nyssa a quick hug. 'Well done, daughter!'

The Doctor was looking up and down the corridor. 'Which way?'

'Follow me, Doctor,' said Nyssa briefly, and led them away.

They hurried through the corridors of the detention area until they came to an intersection.

They heard footsteps coming towards them, and ducked quickly into a side-passage. They stood motionless, flattened against the wall while two patrolling Fosters passed by, and then hurried on their way.

Nyssa led them confidently out of the detention area, along a series of passages, and at last to the antechamber of the Inner Sanctum, where the bodies of Neman and the Foster lay sprawled unconscious.

The Doctor looked at Nyssa and raised an eyebrow. 'Your work, I take it?'

Tremas looked shocked. 'They're not dead, I hope, Nyssa?'

She shook her head, and held up the torch-like device. 'I used your Ion Bonder. I stepped up the ion rate to maximum. They should sleep for quite a bit yet.'

'I must remember not to fall out with your daughter, Tremas,' said the Doctor solemnly. 'Very handy gadget that, young lady. Can I see it?'

Nyssa handed it over, and the Doctor examined it carefully. 'Yes, very clever. No fugitive should be without one.' He slipped it absent-mindedly into his pocket. 'We'd better be getting back to the Grove and into the TARDIS. Much the safest place at the moment.'

'That's why I brought you here,' said Nyssa impatiently. 'You can go through the Sanctum and use the secret passage.'

Suddenly Tremas stared at his hand in dismay. 'But we can't get into the Sanctum. They have taken my ring.'

'Then we'll have to go the other way,' said the Doctor.

'We can't, Doctor,' said Adric. 'The main gate is guarded all the time now.'

'It's still the only way in. Don't worry, Adric, we'll think of something when we get there.'

The sudden clangour of an alarm bell filled the air.

'If we get there, of course,' added the Doctor thoughtfully. 'I think they've just discovered we're missing. Come on!'

8

A Place to Hide

The doors to the Sanctum opened and Luvic and Katura emerged, deep in discussion. 'I still don't like it,' Luvic was saying. 'Think of it—an execution. A most painful duty.'

'Not the Traken way at all, this judicial blood-letting,' agreed Katura. 'Still if it must be, it must. The sooner we get it over with the better.'

These gloomy reflections were interrupted by a low groan.

Looking around in astonishment, Luvic was astounded to see Neman struggling painfully to his feet. 'Proctor Neman! What has happened to you?'

Kassia came hurrying out of the Sanctum, and took in the situation at a glance. 'The prisoners!' she snapped. 'They have escaped?'

Neman nodded painfully. 'We were attacked, Consul. The Lady Nyssa ... she had some kind of weapon. She took my keys ...'

'Search the Court,' ordered Kassia angrily. 'Find them, Neman, or you and all your Fosters will wish you'd never been born!'

'Yes, my lady.'

By now the Foster, too, was on his feet. He staggered out of the anteroom. Neman was about to follow when Kassia snapped, 'Wait!'

'My lady?'

'Seal the entire Court. Double the guards on the Sanctum and on the Grove. Search everywhere—and don't forget the residential quarter.'

'Yes, my lady.' Neman hurried away.

Deciding that speed rather than stealth offered the best chance of escape, the Doctor led his party along the corridors at a run.

They actually ran straight into a pair of patrolling Fosters, but the Doctor and his friends were moving so quickly that they had disappeared around a corner before the astonished Fosters realised what was happening.

Belatedly the Fosters gave chase.

Some time later, the fugitives slowed down a little and listened. The sounds of pursuit seemed to be moving away from them. 'Someone must have taken a wrong turning,' said the Doctor happily. 'We must be nearly there now.'

They reached the end of the corridor, and suddenly two Fosters stepped out in front of them, weapons levelled.

'Afternoon,' said the Doctor politely. 'Or is it still morning? Hard to keep track of time around here, isn't it?'

One of the Fosters raised his weapon. 'Up against the wall, all of you.'

They backed against the wall, the Fosters covering them with their weapons.

'Doctor, the Ion Bonder,' hissed Nyssa.

'Good idea,' said the Doctor. He looked hopefully at the guards. 'Have you ever seen an Ion Bonder?' He began fumbling in his pockets. 'I've got one here, somewhere. Most interesting little gadget.'

'That's enough,' snarled the Foster. 'Don't try to escape or you'll all be killed.'

Ignoring him the Doctor fished out the Ion Bonder and held it in front of him. 'Here it is—just keep your eye on that!' He touched a switch, a green ray shot out and the Foster fell. The Doctor swung the device on the second Foster, and the green ray dropped him beside his fellow. 'Quite a useful little weapon, that,' said the Doctor. 'If you care for that sort of thing!'

'Listen, Doctor!' said Tremas urgently.

They could hear the sounds of pusuit from all around them, shouted orders, the sound of marching footsteps. The hunt was closing in. 'We don't stand a chance in these corridors,' said the Doctor. 'We've got to find somewhere to lie low for a while.'

Nyssa looked at her father. 'Do you realise where we are? We're very close to our own living quarters.'

Tremas looked worried. 'That's too risky, surely? Wouldn't that be the first place they'd look?'

'That's right,' said Adric. 'They've probably searched it already by now!'

'Well said, Adric,' said the Doctor. 'Nothing like the obvious to mislead and confuse. Besides, Tremas and I have some business to transact there.'

'We have, Doctor?'

The Doctor beamed. 'Let's get there first, shall we?'

They moved on their way.

In the Grove, Kassia was desperately trying to excuse herself to Melkur. 'The Doctor and his friends will soon be recaptured, Melkur.'

'I am disappointed, Kassia. You have failed me.'

'We will find them, Melkur. The Court is sealed— they cannot escape.'

'I warned you about the Doctor's cunning, but you chose to ignore me. Now you must suffer!'

Twin beams arced from Melkur's glowing eyes and for a moment Kassia twisted in agony. The beams faded, and she stood zombie-like, all of her original personality burned away, now utterly and completely a creature of Melkur.

'What must I do, Melkur?'

'Find the Doctor! He must be destroyed, and all his companions with him.'

Kassia bowed her head. 'I shall not rest until it is done.'

'Time presses, Consul,' said Melkur. 'The power of the Keeper is almost mine. Only the Doctor can destroy all I have planned. He must be found. Must be, do you hear me?'

Tremas's living quarters were a shambles. Equipment racks had been torn down and their contents thrown all over the floor, books and papers were scattered everywhere, furniture overturned, statues and ornaments smashed.

The Doctor looked round, shaking his head, 'This new regime is really making a mess of things!'

Adric and Nyssa stayed listening by the door. So far there were no sounds of pursuit. It seemed Adric's guess was right. Having searched and ransacked Tremas's quarters, the Fosters had moved elsewhere.

The Doctor turned to Tremas, who was staring at the desolation in stunned dismay. 'Now, what was it I wanted to talk to you about? Oh yes! Master plans, blueprints ... you wouldn't have them here, would you?'

'Plans for what?'

'The master plans for the Source Manipulator. Are they here?'

Tremas hesitated. 'Yes, they are—in the atmosphere safe.'

'Right,' said the Doctor briskly. 'Let's have a look at them.'

Tremas hesitated. 'Doctor ... maintaining the secrecy of the Source Manipulator is a sacred trust.'

'I know that, Tremas. But we must prevent Kassia from becoming Keeper at all costs, and for that we need those plans.'

'I swore an oath!'

'No doubt you did. Now you have to choose. Your personal honour against the safety of all Traken.'

Tremas agonised for a moment longer. 'I can't do it, Doctor!'

'Well done!' said the Doctor. 'So when Melkur has taken control of the Source, you'll have the consolation of knowing your personal honour is intact.'

Nyssa had been listening to all this from her place near the door. She came over to Tremas, and put her hand on his arm. 'The Doctor's right, you know, father.'

Tremas paced to and fro for a moment and then came to a decision. 'Very well!'

He walked over to an apparently blank piece of wall and held his palm flat against it. After a moment, a square of wall began to glow, and then seemed to dissolve altogether. Tremas put his hand inside, and took out an ancient scroll.

He took it over to the table and unrolled it with infinite care. 'There you are, Doctor. The original design of the Source Manipulator, the secret of our Keepers' power.'

*

Kassia strode the corridors of the Court like a fury, harrying and driving the Fosters in their search for the fugitives. At one of the junctions she saw Neman running towards her. He halted, gasping and saluted. 'My lady.'

'Well?'

'No sign of them, Consul. Some of my men made contact, but they lost them again.'

Kassia struck her fist into her palm. 'Where, then? Where can they be?'

'When last seen they were heading towards the Grove.

'Obviously. They were trying to reach the Doctor's space-craft.' Kassia considered. 'Very well, we will make things easy for them, Neman. Call off the search.'

'Call it off, Consul?'

'Yes. Have the Fosters withdrawn, all of them.'

'What about the guards covering the entrance to the Grove.'

'Those especially.'

Neman was puzzled but obedient. 'Very well, Consul it shall be done. May I ask what you have in mind?'

'The death of the Doctor!'

The Doctor completed his study of the Source Manipulator plans, and looked up. 'Magnificent, Tremas! Pity it all depends on some poor chap sitting in that chair for thousands of years—but magnificent, all the same.'

'The life of one man is a small price to pay for harmony throughout all the Traken Union, for thousands of years of peace and prosperity for all our people.'

'Yes, there is that, I suppose,' said the Doctor

absently. He turned to Adric, who was still studying the plan. 'It seems to me that the crucial circuit is ...'

Adric pointed. 'Here?'

'Right. Now the thing is, could it be tripped?'

Adric shuddered. 'I wouldn't like to be anywhere around if it was! The amount of sheer power involved ...'

Tremas was looking horrified. 'May I ask what you have in mind, Doctor.'

The Doctor beamed at him. 'Oh, dangerous thoughts, Tremas. Dangerous thoughts.' He turned back to Adric. 'You see?' His finger moved over the map. 'The warp cross-over connected here ... a shut-off element here and—'

'Disaster!' said Adric

'Well ... only if the servo-mechanisms blew,' said the Doctor calmly. 'Anyway, bear it in mind—just in case!'

'You're not serious, are you, Doctor?'

'Oh yes! It would be tricky, mind you, but not impossible. Still, perhaps it won't be necessary.' Carefully the Doctor rolled up the scroll and handed it to Tremas. 'Thank you, Tremas. You can put it away again now.'

Tremas went back to the glowing square in the wall, put the scroll inside, and passed his hand across the space. The glowing square disappeared, and the wall was just a wall again.

The Doctor looked at Nyssa, who had returned to her watch at the door. 'How are the fun and games outside, Nyssa?'

'Everything's quiet, Doctor. No movement, nothing!'

'Good! I think it's time we had another go at reaching the TARDIS!'

*

In the Inner Sanctum, Katura and Luvic were gazing anxiously into the Keeper's Chamber.

The flame above the throne had been burning low for hours now, flickering, and reviving briefly, only to fail again. A low moaning sound filled the Sanctum.

Sadly Luvic said, 'The signs are unmistakable now, Katura.'

The old woman nodded. 'Yes, it's happening at last.' She turned to the foster at the door. 'Find Consul Kassia, and bring her here immediately.'

The Foster saluted. 'What shall I tell her, my lady?'

'Tell her the Keeper is dying.'

The Doctor and his little group moved cautiously along one of the corridors, heading in the direction of the Grove.

'I don't understand it,' said Nyssa uneasily. 'No Fosters anywhere!'

Adric shrugged. 'Maybe they've called off the search.'

Tremas shook his head. 'It isn't like Kassia to give up so easily. I don't like it.'

'Nor do I,' said the Doctor thoughtfully. He brightened. 'Still, to quote an old Earth proverb, "What can't be cured must be endured!"'

'That's the silliest thing I ever heard,' said Adric in disgust.

The Doctor grinned. 'Oh, don't listen to me. I never do!'

Before very long they had reached the courtyard. There, on the other side, was the entrance to the Grove. Their footsteps echoed in the silence as they crossed the courtyard.

83

Adric looked round uneasily. 'I still don't like it, Doctor.'

'It's very quiet, isn't it? Very quiet indeed. Still, nothing ventured, nothing ...' He caught Adric's eye. 'Oh, never mind. Let's have this gate open then.' He shoved at the massive iron gate.

Adric and Tremas came to help, and the gate swung open. 'It wasn't even locked,' said Adric wonderingly.

Tremas looked worriedly at the Doctor. 'Do you think we should go in?'

'I don't think we have any choice,' said the Doctor gently.

He looked at the others. 'We'll have to pass that statue to reach the TARDIS, so watch out for any funny business. Remember, don't look in its eyes!'

They entered the Grove.

The flame was flickering even more feebly now, and it had burned very low. The Inner Sanctum grew steadily darker, and the electronic howl louder.

'The legends say that it is an agonising death,' whispered Luvic.

Katura bowed her head. 'For the Keeper's sake and ours, may it come swiftly. As the Keeper dies the Source slips out of control, and in the time between Keepers, nature itself reverts to destructive chaos. My dread is that something will go wrong with the transfer.'

'Kassia must be ready the instant the Keeper dies,' said Luvic. 'Then all will be well.'

Katura looked anxiously towards the door. 'She must hurry. Time is running out!'

*

As always these days, the atmosphere in the Grove seemed heavy, menacing. Even the rustling and crackling of the plants had something sinister about it.

They were nearing the clearing that held the TARDIS—and Melkur—when Adric said, 'Wait. Listen. I'm sure I heard someone.'

They paused, listening. For a moment there seemed to be a crackle of stealthy movement ahead—then all was silent again.

The Doctor was about to beckon them forward when suddenly a line of armed Fosters rose out of the undergrowth ahead of them. They turned to run—but more Fosters had appeared behind, and on either side.

They were surrounded.

Proctor Neman appeared from behind his men, a look of grim satisfaction on his face.

The Doctor nodded. 'Well, well, you seem to have made a very good recovery!'

'Unfortunately for you, Doctor. Stand very still.'

Ignoring the command, Tremas stepped forward. 'Proctor Neman! I am Tremas, one of your Consuls. What has happened to you and your people?'

For a moment Neman seemed moved by the appeal, then he held up his hand. 'Be silent, Consul. There is nothing more to be said. My instructions are clear.'

'Well, clarity is the soul of knowing what the other fellow's up to,' said the Doctor obscurely. 'So, what are you up to, Neman?'

Neman raised his voice. 'By order of the Keeper-Nominate you are all declared to be traitors to Traken, and sentenced to death. Sentence will be carried out immediately. Fosters!'

The Fosters behind the Doctor and his group moved to one side. Those in front formed into a ragged line, a kind of impromptu firing squad.

'Fire on my command,' shouted Nemàn.

He raised his hand.

The Fosters levelled their guns.

9

Death of a Keeper

The Grove exploded.

The sun went dark, a weird electronic sobbing filled the air, lightning flashed, there were deafening claps of thunder, and a hurricane-like wind lashed through the trees.

'What's happening, Tremas?' yelled the Doctor.

Tremas clutched his arm. 'The Keeper, Doctor! The Keeper is dying.'

The Fosters were terrified. They turned and fled, crashing away through the wind-lashed shrubbery, some of them dropping their blasters in their panic.

Only Neman made a last attempt to do what he saw as his duty. He snatched up a fallen blaster and aimed it at the little group. But the Doctor's hand was already coming out of his pocket, and he shot Neman down with the Ion Bonder before he could fire. Neman crumpled and fell.

The Doctor looked round. Nyssa had been blown literally off her feet and was struggling to rise. 'Help her, Adric,' shouted the Doctor.

Adric pulled Nyssa upright.

Tremas was staring wide-eyed at the howling desolation all around him. 'He dies—the Keeper dies!'

The Doctor shook him by the shoulders. 'Yes—and Kassia will be the next Keeper if we don't get a move on. We must get to the Sanctum!'

Struggling against the driving wind, they staggered away.

By now even the Inner Sanctum was being scoured by the howling winds.

Katura and Luvic were flattened against the wall, striving desperately to keep on their feet.

The only light now came from the flickering, ebbing flame, casting nightmarish shadows around the walls of the Sanctum.

The door flew open with a crash and Kassia stood in the doorway, eyes gleaming.

'Kassia, come quickly,' shouted Luvic.

Kassia strode up to the foot of the steps to the Keeper's Chamber. For a moment her eyes glowed redly and she whispered, 'Yes, Melkur. The time has come.'

In the control room, the hooded figure could see her face on the twin screens, hear her whispering voice. 'The Source is almost out of control. Soon it will be ours!'

The figure leaned forward and hissed, 'Do what must be done, Kassia. I am impatient.'

In the storm-swept Sanctum, Kassia mounted the Chamber steps and spoke directly to the guttering flame. 'Keeper of Traken, your task is done. Go swiftly, with our gratitude for all you have accomplished. She who is to succeed you is present and waiting. Relinquish the Source, and die!'

The wind dropped.

The electronic howling faded into silence.

The flame of the Source flared higher for one brief moment—then went out.

Katura gasped, and clutched at Luvic's arm. 'He is gone!'

The Chamber doors slid back and Kassia entered.

The Doctor and his friends were still crossing the Grove when the sudden silence fell. 'He is gone,' whispered Tremas. 'The Keeper is dead!'

'Swiftly now,' said the Doctor. 'No time to lose.' They hurried on.

Kassia sat proudly on the Keeper's throne, with Luvic and Katura looking up at her.

Above the throne, the flame-holder was still empty, dead.

'There is no flame,' whispered Luvic. 'Has the Source survived?'

'All will be well,' said Katura soothingly. 'All will now be as it should be.' But her voice trembled and there was fear in her eyes.

The doors to the Chamber slid closed.

Luvic and Katura moved closer.

It was very dark in the Sanctum now that the flame was gone, but inside the transparent walls of the Keeper's Chamber, the figure of Kassia began to glow.

Muffled a little but still quite audible, her voice came from within the Chamber. 'Consuls, you are witness to my acceptance. Instruct the Source so that transition may be effected.'

The Doctor, Adric, Nyssa and Tremas were nearing the secret exit from the Grove when they heard a soft, eerie voice behind them.

'Doctor!'

They turned.

Melkur stood at the edge of the clearing behind them, eyes glowing redly. 'So, Doctor, you survive after all?'

'Yes, we're still around. Don't write us off yet, will you?'

'Look into my eyes, all of you!'

'Oh no!' shouted the Doctor.

'There is nothing more you can do, Doctor. Look into my eyes and you will die swiftly—a merciful death. Refuse, and you will regret it.'

'We know what you're up to Melkur—and we're going to stop you, that's a promise.'

'But it is too late, Doctor. The Source is mine!'

In the Sanctum the silver band around Kassia's neck glowed bright. Suddenly the flame sprang into life, burning steady and tall.

Taking care not to look into the eyes of Melkur, the Doctor spread out his arms and herded his group away. 'Careful now! Don't look back—and whatever you do, don't look into his eyes.'

The mocking voice of Melkur followed him. 'The Source is mine, Doctor. And soon, very soon, you will feel its power.'

The twin screens showed the Doctor and his party at the entrance to the tunnel that led to the storage vault. As they filed inside the hooded creature reached out and touched a control, and the screens went dead.

Swivelling round in his chair, the hooded figure surveyed his domain, a darkly opulent control room,

90

furnished not in white but in gleaming black. Against one wall stood the incongruous shape of an old-fashioned grandfather clock, its ticks measuring the silence.

The figure in the chair was both wizened and decayed, the body as worn out as the tattered robes. One eye glared madly from the crumbling ruin of a face and blackened lips drew back in a ghastly chuckle. 'Now this Traken web of harmony is broken—and I am free!' Swinging back to face the console he stretched out a claw-like hand.

As the door closed behind the Doctor's little party, a curious wheezing groaning sound filled the air. But the blue police box stayed exactly where it was, in the Grove. It was the statue of Melkur that dematerialised.

The control console at the base of the Keeper's Chamber contained an elaborate digital keyboard. Katura knelt beside it, tapping out a complex numerical sequence.

She looked up at Kassia, who sat statue-like in the throne. 'By this key-code, Kassia, you are physically confirmed as Keeper. Prepare for access to the Source. May you bring peace and blessings to Traken for all your time, Keeper.'

As Katura prepared to key in the last numbers in the code-sequence, the Doctor dashed out of the door that led to the vaults, with Tremas, Nyssa and Adric close behind him. 'Consul Katura—don't do it!' shouted the Doctor.

Katura was furious at the interruption. 'You again, Doctor!'

Luvic came forward, his voice trembling with

indignation. 'Fosters, these traitors have no business here!'

Angry Fosters moved forwards to bar the Doctor's way.

'Listen to me,' said the Doctor urgently. 'Consul Kassia has betrayed you all. *Don't complete the transition!*'

Kassia's voice came from within the Chamber. 'Consul Katura! Do your duty!'

The Doctor struggled to force his way past the Fosters. 'Don't listen to her!'

'*Complete the transition!*' screamed Kassia.

'No, Katura,' shouted Tremas. 'Don't do it!'

Katura hesitated. She looked from Tremas to the Doctor, then up at the figure of Kassia.

She leaned forward, keyed in the last numbers of the code-sequence, and then threw a switch. 'Transition is complete, Keeper. You have access to the Source!'

The Chamber filled with light, and Kassia's body began to twist and shudder, her face distorted with agony. Her body shimmered, became transparent, and faded slowly from sight.

The Keeper's throne was empty.

'The Keeper,' whispered Luvic fearfully. 'What has happened to the Keeper?'

A giant form began to materialise inside the Chamber.

The Doctor looked round. The eyes of everyone in the room were fixed on the Keeper's throne.

He edged closer to Adric. 'Quick, this is your only chance. Take Nyssa to the TARDIS. Wait for me there.'

'What about you, Doctor?'

'There may still be something I can do here.'

'But Doctor—'

'Don't argue, Adric. Get to the TARDIS. And if all else fails remember our plan!'

Adric moved over to Nyssa and took her by the hand. Putting a finger to his lips he led her quietly to the storage-vault door. No one even noticed them leave.

The Doctor turned his attention back to the Chamber. The form was almost fully materialised by now. Tremas gave a gasp of horror and took a step towards it, but the Doctor held him back. 'Don't go near it, Tremas. It's too late now. Far too late.'

Seconds later the materialisation was complete. Before them, in the Keeper's throne, sat Melkur.

10

The Rule of Melkur

No one stirred.

Then Melkur spoke.

The voice was deep and sibilant, and at the same time curiously gentle. 'My thanks to you, Consul Katura. You were wise to complete my access to the Source. I am grateful.'

'Who are you?' asked Katura fearfully. 'What are you?'

'Haven't you realised?' said the Doctor. 'This is your new Keeper.'

Tremas was horrified. 'This is no Keeper of Traken!'

'Not quite what you had in mind, I know. But now I'm afraid you're rather stuck with him.'

In the same gentle voice Melkur said 'Consul Luvic, you may now summon Proctor Neman.'

Luvic stared up at the Chamber, too horrified to move.

'You'd better do it, Consul,' advised the Doctor. 'Otherwise he'll make you.'

'There is no compulsion,' said Melkur mildly. 'It is your Keeper who asks—do it to serve him.'

'No compulsion?' mocked the Doctor. 'You've changed your tune.'

'But apparently you have not, Doctor.' The great stone head turned towards Katura and Luvic. 'This man is known to me, Consuls, as is his ambition—to seize control of the Source!'

'Rubbish,' said the Doctor vigorously. 'My only ambition is to put a stop to you.'

'An unhappy man,' sighed Melkur. 'You will remember, Consuls, that the old Keeper rejected him. You yourselves sentenced him to death, is that not so?'

'It is the truth,' said Katura. 'Luvic, obey the Keeper.'

Luvic stumbled from the Sanctum.

The Doctor edged closer to Tremas. 'You know there's something very familiar about Melkur. Not so much the appearance as the manner. I keep thinking I've met him somewhere before. If only I could get a closer look . . .'

Adric and Nyssa hurried along the passage, through the storage vault, past the great glowing globe of the Source Manipulator, along the tunnel and up the steps, and out into the Grove, now quiet and peaceful again.

When they came to the central clearing, the TARDIS was still there. But Melkur had gone.

Nyssa shivered. 'How could it just disappear and reappear like that?'

'Oh that's nothing, we do it all the time in the TARDIS.' Adric paused, realising the significance of what he had just said. 'No wonder those energy profiles looked so familiar.'

Nyssa gave him a baffled look. 'Adric, what are you saying?'

'I'm saying Melkur must be a kind of TARDIS too . . .' Adric produced his TARDIS key. 'We'd better get inside.' He paused, looking at Nyssa thoughtfully. 'I'd better warn you—you're in for a bit of a shock!'

*

Tremas was trying vainly to argue with Melkur. 'You have no right to sit on that throne!'

'I have every right. It is by the will of your last Keeper that I am here.'

'Do you really expect us to believe you were known to the old Keeper?'

'Known to him? I tell you, Consul Tremas, it was he who arranged that I should succeed him.'

'Impossible,' said Tremas firmly. 'No outsider can become Keeper of Traken.'

Katura had been following the argument with keen interest. 'That is true. After all, the Keeper's original choice was Consul Tremas. When Tremas proved unfitting, we ourselves chose Consul Kassia.'

A tinge of impatience came into Melkur's voice. 'The Keeper realised that his choice of Tremas had been an error. That is why it happened as you saw it happen. The old Keeper foresaw all this. Kassia gave her life willingly so that I could serve you.'

All this time, the Doctor had been edging up the steps, and by now he was very close to the figure on the throne.

But the great head was still turned a little away from him. The Doctor decided on a little deliberate provocation. 'Nonsense! If you ask me, poor old Kassia didn't have any choice about it.'

The great head swung round and the slitted eyes stared deep into the Doctor's own. 'Still you do not recognise me!' said that oddly familiar voice. 'But soon you will know me, Doctor. Soon!'

Katura looked accusingly at the Doctor. 'For all we know, you are the cause of this! There were five Consuls before you came! Five!'

The Doctor said, 'I'd be willing to bet that soon there won't be any, the way he's going about things.'

Melkur said mildly, 'My only purpose, Doctor, is to help these people fulfil their destiny. Together, we shall work to achieve my aims.'

'And what might they be? Enslavement, extermination, conquest? That kind of thing?'

Melkur ignored him. 'I am concerned not only with the destiny of Traken, Doctor, but with your own—which will be quite different!'

Bursting with unanswered questions, Nyssa looked on impatiently, while Adric checked over the TARDIS console, throwing a complicated sequence of switches. His task completed, he looked up. 'We're safe now, I think. The door's sealed, the defence shields are up. No one can possibly get in except the Doctor.' Adric looked dubiously at the TARDIS console. 'At least, that's the theory.'

Nyssa looked around the huge control room. 'How can all this be like Melkur?'

'I don't know—but I think it is, all the same.'

'And why is it bigger on the inside than on the outside?'

Adric grinned. 'The Doctor always says "Because it's dimensionally transcendental."'

'And what does that mean?'

Adric grinned, recalling the Doctor's inevitable answer. 'It means it's bigger on the inside than on the outside.'

He moved round the console and began operating controls. The console hummed with life and the big central column began moving slowly up and down.

Nyssa looked alarmed. 'What are you doing?'

'Just testing the drive systems—in case we have to leave in a hurry.'

Suddenly the power hum cut out, and the central column stopped moving.

Puzzled, Adric went through the operational procedures again with exactly the same result.

The TARDIS started up, ran for a while, and then stopped.

Adric frowned and scratched his head. 'We seem to be getting some kind of blocking.'

'Blocking? What does that mean?'

'It means that if we do have to take off in a hurry—we're in very serious trouble.'

By now the Sanctum was getting quite crowded. Proctor Neman was there, and his men, now all re-armed, were lining the walls and guarding the doors.

The giant stone figure of Melkur still occupied the throne. Astonishingly enough, the Trakens actually seemed to be getting used to their extraordinary new Keeper.

Perhaps Melkur's determinedly calm and reasonable tones had a lot to do with it, thought the Doctor.

At the moment, Melkur was addressing Proctor Neman. 'You will dismiss the Consuls and have them confined to their quarters.' Katura started to protest, and Melkur said smoothly, 'A purely temporary measure, I assure you, designed for your own protection.'

Neman shot the Doctor a malevolent glance. 'And the Doctor? He is under sentence of death, Keeper.' Neman looked as if it would give him the greatest of pleasure to carry out the sentence on the spot.

'Yes,' said Melkur gloatingly. 'Sentence of death. I had not forgotten ...' Suddenly the voice seemed to fade, and the Doctor saw that Melkur was beginning to blur a little. I am loathe to begin my new regime with bloodshed,' said Melkur feebly. 'Though in this case the temptation is great!' The voice faltered and when it spoke again it was with a sense of painful effort. 'You will be confined to Court, like the others, Doctor. Your fate will be decided later. Attempt to leave, try to reach the TARDIS, and you will bring suffering upon your friends and upon yourself.'

Melkur faded away.

Proctor Neman looked uncertainly at the empty throne for a moment and then said, 'Doctor, you will be confined with Consul Tremas in his quarters until further notice.'

'Listen to me, Neman. If you serve Melkur he will eventually destroy you,' said the Doctor. 'Just as he destroyed Consul Kassia.'

For a moment Neman looked worried, then he snapped, 'Consuls, you are dismissed. Fosters, escort them to their quarters!'

As they were ushered from the Sanctum, Tremas fell into the step beside Luvic. 'After all that has happened, with that ... thing installed as Keeper, can you still believe me to be a traitor?'

Luvic was still in a state of shock. 'Who knows what to think any more?'

The Doctor said, 'I shouldn't worry about that, Luvic. Pretty soon Melkur will be doing all your thinking for you.'

Outside the antechamber the group was separated, Katura and Luvic led one way, the Doctor and Tremas another.

As the Fosters marched them along the corridor Tremas whispered, 'Doctor, there is still the Ultimate Sanction.'

'There is?'

'If the Consuls decide a Keeper is unfit for his post, we have the authority and the means to cancel his existence.'

'That sounds like a very interesting proposition, Tremas. Tell me more!'

By the time Tremas completed his explanation they were nearly at Tremas's quarters. 'Of course, it requires the unanimous assent of all the Consuls, Doctor!'

'Couldn't be simpler. After all, there are only three left now—and that includes you.'

'Ah, but the procedure calls for the use of all five consular rings.' Tremas looked ruefully down at his hand. 'Kassia must have taken mine, and I imagine she took Seron's too.'

'So presumably Melkur's got them by now.' The Doctor rubbed his chin. 'It's an interesting problem, but not an insoluble one, surely.'

'There's one other thing, Doctor.'

'What?'

'The procedure requires the consent of the Keeper himself.'

'Ah,' said the Doctor thoughtfully. 'That rather knocks the idea on the head, doesn't it?'

By now they were at the door to Treman's quarters. The Fosters opened it and thrust them inside, leaving two or their number behind on guard.

The apartment was still in its semi-wrecked state, and the Doctor gazed sadly around him, shaking his head. 'Looks like a demonstration of the second law of thermodynamics.'

The two Fosters looked impassively at him, and took up positions by the door. The Doctor drew Tremas to one side. 'Speaking of entropy, what do you think was happening back there in the Sanctum? I could have sworn old Melkur was . . . struggling. It seemed to take

100

him a lot of effort to stay in control ... all very unexpected.'

'Not at all, Doctor, it's quite normal. When a new Keeper succeeds there is an initial period of reaction. The effort of taking control of the Source can weaken him dangerously. At first his new powers ... come and go!'

'Do they now? So that's it—reaction. And that's why Melkur is being all sweetness and reason ... because he's vulnerable!'

Tremas nodded. 'I imagine he is postponing any real clash until his power is secure!'

'So perhaps there might be some way of working this Ultimate Sanction thing after all ...'

'Remember, Doctor, his powers are increasing by the minute. The whole reaction process is usually over in a matter of hours.'

The Doctor rubbed his hands.

'But it's possible. It is just *possible*!'

Tremas began to look hopeful, then became crestfallen again. 'What am I thinking of? We'd still need all five rings—and the Keeper's consent!'

The Doctor glanced at the Fosters and then lowered his voice. 'Even though we have the plans of the Source Manipulator?'

Tremas stood quite still for a moment, but his mind was racing. 'Yes ... yes, there could be a way ... If we short-circuit the security system. But we'll have to work quickly, Doctor ...'

Casually, the Doctor and Tremas began wandering towards the point in the wall that concealed the vacuum safe.

Melkur reappeared in the Keeper's chair as suddenly as

he had vanished, and promptly summoned Neman to report to him. 'You have carried out my orders?'

'Yes, Keeper. All Consuls are confined to their quarters and the residential wing is sealed off.'

'Good!' said Melkur mildly. 'My power is not fully active as yet, and until it is I shall depend on you greatly, Proctor Neman. He held out his hand. On it lay a consular ring. Proudly Neman took it and put it on.

'You may count on me, Keeper.'

'I'm sure I can,' said Melkur silkily. 'But just to be entirely sure I have another gift for you. You will find a silver necklet at my feet. Pick it up and put it on.'

Not daring to disobey, Neman stooped and picked up the silver circlet, and placed it around his neck. It seemed to fuse shut and tighten a little, and he felt as if he would never be able to take it off.

Melkur's eyes glowed red. 'Excellent! Let me entrust you with another task, Proctor Neman. Consul Tremas has a certain important document in his possession. It must be secured at once!'

Fortunately the vacuum safe was just out of sight of the door, concealed by a turn of the wall, and Tremas was able to remove the Source Manipulator plans without arousing the curiosity of the Fosters.

The Doctor and Tremas pored over the ancient scroll spread out on the table.

'As you see, Doctor,' Tremas was saying, 'the control panel at the base of the Chamber can only be activated by the five consular rings—'

'Which we have not got,' completed the Doctor. He studied the scroll. 'What's this mechanism here? Oh yes, I see, a recursive integrator.' The Doctor was thinking hard. 'Wait a minute Doctor how are the

Consular rings encoded?'

'By gamma mode encryption.'

'Then in that case, there will be a single large prime number as the code root.'

'Well?'

'Don't you see? If we punched that number into the Chamber control console it would have exactly the same effect as if we used all five rings—and it would by-pass the need for the Keeper's consent as well.' The Doctor frowned. 'Trouble is, we don't know the key integer. Pity you haven't still got your own ring.'

'Oh, you couldn't derive the prime number from just one ring, Doctor. The computations would take thousands of years.'

'I happen to have a bit of a knack for mental arithmetic,' said the Doctor modestly. 'And I do know one or two short cuts . . .' He broke off as the door was flung open and Proctor Neman appeared. 'How nice,' said the Doctor. 'Do come in!'

Neman strode into the room. 'Consul Tremas, I have orders from the Keeper to secure the plan of the Source Manipulator. You will please hand it over.'

Tremas looked worriedly at the Doctor, and saw to his astonishment that the plan had vanished. The Doctor was standing with his hands behind his back, and an innocent expression on his face and Tremas guessed he must be concealing the scroll.

Tremas moved forward, hoping to distract Neman's attention. 'That is impossible, Proctor Neman. The plans of the Source Manipulator are for consular eyes only.'

Neman's hand went to the silver circlet at his neck. 'The Keeper orders it. That is reason enough.' Neman drew his weapon, and levelled it at Tremas's head. 'You will do as I say.'

Tremas shook his head. 'I cannot.'

There was a strange, wheezing, groaning noise, a shimmering in the air, and suddenly Melkur appeared, seated in his Keeper's throne in the centre of the room.

'Dear me,' said the Doctor to himself. 'He seems almost back on form.'

Melkur spoke. 'Consul Tremas, you will do as Proctor Neman asks.'

'No,' said Tremas defiantly. 'I tell you as I told him—'

Twin beams lanced from Melkur's eyes, and Tremas collapsed, writhing in agony.

11

The Last Resort

The Doctor knew he must act quickly to save Tremas's life.

'All right, all right!' he shouted. 'We'll give you the plans.' He went and helped Tremas to his feet. 'No need to show off your new powers, Melkur, we know what you can do.'

He settled the shaken Tremas in a chair.

'That was only a beginning, Doctor. You do well to persuade your friend to co-operate.'

The Doctor put a hand on Tremas's shoulder. 'Do as he says, Tremas. It's only a piece of paper after all.'

'But Doctor ...'

'Anyway he doesn't actually want it for himself. Melkur knows all about the Source by now. He just wants to make sure you don't show it to me. Isn't that right, Melkur?'

'That is correct, Doctor. Once you had seen those plans, I should have no alternative but to execute you immediately.'

'Afraid I might spoil your fun, eh?' The Doctor helped Tremas to his feet and led him over to the wall safe, quickly passing the rolled-up scroll to him in the process.

By keeping his body between Tremas and Melkur,

the Doctor enabled Tremas to open the vacuum safe and pretend to remove the scroll.

With a great show of reluctance, Tremas held out the plans, and Neman snatched them from him.

Suddenly Melkur blurred and then reappeared.

The Doctor laughed. 'I'd watch it if I were you, Melkur. You've been burning the candle at both ends!'

'Neman! Hold up the scroll,' ordered Melkur.

Neman obeyed. Tremas's eyes widened at the sight of the consular ring on his finger.

Twin beams shot from Melkur's eyes, blasting the scroll into smoking ash.

'Now I am safe, Doctor,' said Melkur painfully. 'The Source is secure!'

He slumped back, and seconds later both Melkur and the throne disappeared.

The Doctor decided it was time for action. 'Neman, come here a minute,' he called. 'I've got something to tell you—something your precious Melkur doesn't know.' He turned to the Fosters. 'This will interest you chaps too.'

At a nod from Neman, the two Fosters came closer.

The Doctor lowered his voice to a confidential murmur. 'I've been telling my friend Adric about these old Earth proverbs. Well, there's one that goes, "*Two heads are better than one*".'

With that the Doctor sprang forward, arms spread wide, grabbed each Foster by the scruff of the neck and slammed their heads together. Before Neman could react, the Doctor hurled both bodies at him, and their combined weights bore him to the ground. Neman scrambled to his feet his blaster in his hand—only to collapse again as Tremas slammed a heavy instrument case down on his head.

Quickly the Doctor knelt down and patted Neman's

tunic until he found the Ion Bonder which he slipped into his own pocket. 'I'm getting quite fond of this.'

Tremas meanwhile was tugging his consular ring from Neman's finger. 'Well, that's at least part of the problem solved, Doctor.'

'Yes, it's going splendidly, isn't it? Judging by the way Melkur looked just then he'll be out of action for a while. Let's see what we can do to make it a more permanent arrangement!'

He opened the door and they slipped out into the corridor—and walked straight into two patrolling Fosters.

Tremas prepared to turn and run but the Doctor whispered, 'Keep walking. See if we can bluff it out.'

As they drew level, the two Foster's drew their blasters. 'Halt!' shouted the nearest.

Tremas said haughtily, 'I am Consul Tremas on a special mission for the Keeper.'

The Doctor and Tremas walked straight past, and for a moment it seemed as if the plan had worked.

Then one of the Fosters shouted, 'Halt or we fire. No one may leave the residential quarter!'

'Pity,' said the Doctor, and turned round, the Ion Bonder in his hand. He fired twice, and both Fosters dropped. The Doctor pointed to a nearby doorway. 'Quick, get them in there.'

They shoved the unconscious bodies out of sight, and hurried on.

Some time later they emerged into a courtyard, only to see two more Fosters strolling towards them. Ignoring them, the Doctor and Tremas walked calmly on. The Fosters looked suspiciously at them, but made no move to stop them.

'That makes a nice change,' whispered the Doctor.

'Maybe it's because we're out of the residential

quarter,' said Tremas. 'Come on, there's still quite a way to go.'

In the TARDIS, Nyssa was pacing up and down. Adric was still working, this time on a complex piece of equipment which he was assembling with spare parts from the TARDIS's storage locker.

He'd been working for quite some time now and had filled a large sphere with electronic circuitry. The whole set-up was fixed to a kind of base plate. An open tool-box stood beside him. At last Nyssa burst out, 'If you'd only tell me what you're doing!'

'You wouldn't like it.'

'Try me!'

Adric went on working. 'The Doctor showed me how Melkur could be destroyed. A kind of last resort if all else failed.'

'How?'

'With this thing—it's a kind of circuit-breaker.'

'What does it do?'

'You won't like it, I tell you.'

'Adric, if it destroys Melkur—'

'Trouble is, it'll do rather more than that.'

'What do you mean?'

'We can stop Melkur, Nyssa, even now. But only by completely destroying the Source.'

Nyssa was too shocked to speak.

Adric completed a circuit connection and straightened up. 'There's the servo shut-off.' Wearily he rubbed his hand over his eyes.

'You'd better let me help you,' said Nyssa. She fished an electronic screwdriver from the tool box.

'Thanks. There's just the cross-over element left . . .'

*

Neman got groggily to his feet, realised that his prisoners were gone and staggered down the corridor in pursuit.

Some way on, he heard a muffled groaning, opened a storeroom door and dragged out a semi-conscious Foster. Brutally he shook the man into wakefulness. 'Which way were they heading?'

'That way ... towards the Sanctum.'

Letting the man slump back, Neman broke into a run.

The Doctor and Tremas walked boldly into the Sanctum antechamber. Two more Fosters were guarding the main doors. Tremas waved them aside. 'Orders from Proctor Neman. We are summoned to the Keeper.'

Tremas put his ring-stone into the locking device and the doors slid open.

As the Doctor and Tremas walked calmly through, a voice shouted, 'Stop them!'

The Fosters turned to see Neman running towards them, blaster in hand.

'Stop them!' screamed Neman again. He fired, but the shot went wild.

The Fosters turned to pursue the fugitives, but the Sanctum door closed in their faces, just as Neman came running up.

Neman looked down at his ringless hand, and slammed an angry fist against the door.

The Doctor and Tremas stood looking round the Sanctum. The Chamber was empty and the flickering light of the flame sent their shadows dancing eerily around the room.

They went over to the control console in the side of the Chamber. Tremas removed a panel to reveal a maze of complex circuitry beneath. The Doctor studied it thoughtfully.

'How long do we have, Tremas?'

'Impossible to say. Not long. The next time we see Melkur, the reaction period will almost certainly be over.' As he spoke, Tremas took a small torch-like instrument from his pocket, and began passing it to and fro over the circuitry. It gave out a low humming sound. Tremas listened carefully to each minute variation in pitch.

The Doctor said thoughtfully. 'I did consider a more drastic approach ... but it won't be necessary now.'

'You know another way to destroy Melkur?'

'Oh, just an idea I was discussing with Adric.'

Tremas's instrument gave a series of high-pitched beeps.

Tremas smiled. 'Progress, Doctor. We're ready for your code-breaking now.'

Tremas inserted his ring-stone in the appropriate slot, and a series of numbers appeared on the read-out section of the console. The Doctor looked thoughtfully at them. These were the first digits of the prime number that formed the key-code. All he had to do now was find the other digits. To help him, he had Tremas and his electronic search key. The variations in pitch would tell them whether the numbers the Doctor entered were hot or cold—right, nearly right, or utterly wrong. But Tremas could only provide a series of clues and indications. To deduce the entire prime number would call for brilliant mathematical calculations and a large element of luck.

Patiently, the Doctor and Tremas set to work.

Adric made a final connection and sat back, mopping his brow.

'Finished?' asked Nyssa sympathetically.

He nodded. 'All we have to do now is connect this circuit-breaker to the Source Manipulator circuits.'

'What will it do?'

'Nothing—until Melkur tries to tap the energy-core of the Source.'

'What happens then?'

'All sorts of things. Time and energy will be displaced, and the energy flow will reverse and overload the control element.'

'What about Melkur?'

'According to the Doctor, the Source will consume itself and whoever controls it. At least, that's the theory.'

'Well,' said Nyssa, 'there's only one way to put it to the test.'

The Doctor and Tremas were working feverishly. After a slow start they had had a sudden run of success, as digit after digit fell into place. Now it seemed that they might actually succeed in finding the code number after all.

'Go on, Doctor,' said Tremas. 'Go on!'

The Doctor was working at frantic speed now, using a method compounded of calculation, intuition and sheer guesswork. 'Eight, eight, seven, one, zero ... another zero ...'

Suddenly light fell upon the console. The Doctor looked up. The Chamber above them was beginning to

111

glow. 'Oh dear, that's a bad sign ... I think Melkur's back!'

In the Chamber above them, the image of Melkur was beginning to form. 'Keep low, Tremas,' whispered the Doctor. 'He isn't fully materialised yet. We may just do it. Only three digits to go ...'

The Doctor studied the row of numbers across the digital read-out screen—and in a sudden intuitive flash he saw what the last three numbers must be.

He reached out to punch them in—and suddenly a section of wall exploded, blowing him away from the console. He scrambled to his feet and there was a second explosion, closer this time.

A peal of satanic laughter filled the Sanctum. The Doctor looked up.

Melkur sat in the Chamber on the Keeper's throne, fully materialised and radiating power, his eyes glowing red. Melkur laughed again, and suddenly a whirlwind sprang up around Tremas and the Doctor, spinning them around like leaves in an autumn gale and then smashing them to the ground.

Painfully the Doctor raised his head. 'Tremas, can you hear me?'

An agonised whisper came back. 'Did you key in ... whole number?'

'Not quite ... three digits to go.'

'We almost had the Sanction Program running ... a matter of moments, Doctor.'

'Listen, Tremas, there's still a chance. I know those last digits. Three ... three ... seven. Remember, three, three, seven.

Suddenly an invisible force plucked the Doctor to his feet.

'Let's have you closer, Doctor, shall we?' said a gloating voice.

The Doctor found himself mounting the steps until he stood before the terrifying figure on the throne.

'And now an attitude of proper respect, I think, Doctor,' said the silky voice.

The Doctor exerted all his strength and all his will, but slowly, inch by inch, he was forced to his knees.

Melkur threw back his head and gave a great howl of laughter. 'You see, Doctor, you cannot stand against me now. I control the Source!'

12

The Enemy

The Grove was silent and deserted as Adric and Nyssa, carrying the circuit-breaker between them, came out of the TARDIS and headed for the entrance to the tunnel.

They went down the steps, along the corridor and into the vault. There they deposited the apparatus beside the glowing globe of the Source Manipulator.

To Nyssa's horror, the Source Manipulator was pulsing with life, dark shapes swirling about in its interior. 'Adric, I think we may be too late. Look at the Source. Melkur must be active.'

'I need access to the prime circuit. Quickly, Nyssa!'

Nyssa touched a switch and a panel slid back, revealing a mass of glowing circuitry.

Adric looked dubiously at it, and even more dubiously at the improvised piece of equipment he had brought with him.

'D'you know how to connect it up?' asked Nyssa.

'I think so.' Adric sighed. 'At least—I hope so.' He set to work.

Summoning up all his courage, Tremas came to stand behind the kneeling Doctor. 'You may call yourself Keeper of Traken, Melkur, but our people will never accept you!'

'A noble sentiment,' said Melkur mockingly. 'But quite untrue, I fear. Your people will obey me—just as you will.'

'I would die rather than serve you.'

Suddenly Tremas lunged towards the console—only to find himself frozen in mid-movement. 'That really isn't necessary,' said Melkur mildly.

Step by step, Tremas found himself moving away from the console, until he was standing before the Chamber, looking up at Melkur. 'Now, Consul Tremas—tell me, who do you obey?'

Slowly, painfully, each word forced from unwilling lips, Tremas said, 'I obey you, Melkur.'

'Let us put it to the test, shall we?'

The Sanctum door flew open with a crash, revealing an astonished Neman.

'Enter, Proctor Neman.'

Neman walked slowly forward to stand beside Tremas.

'Please hand your energy-weapon to Consul Tremas.'

Moving as if of its own accord, Neman's hand drew the blaster and held it out.

Equally unwillingly, Tremas's hand came out and took it.

With a supreme effort, the Doctor rose to his feet. He took a step towards Tremas, and found himself frozen where he stood by Melkur's will.

'You may watch, but not interfere, Doctor. Now, Neman, you failed in your duty to me, did you not?'

Great drops of sweat rolled down Neman's forehead, but he could not move his hand to brush them away. 'I tried, Keeper.'

'But you failed,' said Melkur gently. 'The punishment for failure is death. You're a fair-minded man,

Consul Tremas, I'm sure you want to see justice done. Kindly destroy Proctor Neman for me will you?'

The blaster in Tremas's hand seemed to rise of its own accord until it was levelled at Neman's heart.

Neman wanted to run, but he could not move.

Tremas felt his finger tightening on the trigger. The gun fired—and Neman stood motionless. Then, released from the power of Melkur at last, he fell to the ground.

Tremas looked down at the body, shuddering with horror. He tried to swing the gun round and turned inwards, until it was pointing at his own head.

'And now yourself, Consul Tremas,' said the gentle voice.

Tremas felt his finger tightening on the trigger.

Suddenly Melkur laughed, and the gun was plucked from his fingers to fly spinning into the darkness.

'You see?' said Melkur triumphantly. 'You will accept me as Keeper. You will all accept me. You no longer have any choice.'

Nyssa watched tensely as Adric made the last delicate connection and locked it in place. 'That's it.'

'Brilliant, Adric. My father couldn't have done it better!'

Adric moved cautiously to the door that led to the Sanctum and opened it.

They heard Melkur's voice.

'Yes, Tremas, you will build great machines—to my design, of course. Your colleagues will mobilise the people of the Traken Union to my service, and I shall lead them to the conquest of worlds without number.'

116

'Same old delusions of grandeur,' said the Doctor wearily.

Melkur said savagely, 'Yes—and many old scores will be settled along the way.'

'Old scores?'

'Can it be that you still do not know me, Doctor?'

From the corner of his eye, the Doctor saw Adric and Nyssa emerge from the storage vault.

He waved his hand warningly behind him, and they drew back into the shadows.

Melkur was still boasting of his coming glory. 'And all this will be as nothing when I come to control the deepest mysteries of time!'

The Doctor raised his voice. 'That too? And how do you propose going about it?'

'Through you—Time Lord! The knowledge will be taken from you, atom by atom. And when nothing is left of you but the husk of your body, that too will have its uses.'

Suddenly the Doctor felt himself drawn towards the Chamber. He tried to back away, but it was useless. An unseen force was drawing him remorselessly forward.

Melkur laughed. 'There is nowhere left to hide now—Time Lord.'

As Adric and Nyssa came rushing out of the shadows, the Doctor was drawn into the Chamber and the transparent walls closed upon him.

For a moment the Doctor and Melkur were in the Chamber together—then both disappeared.

Instinctively Tremas rushed towards the digital console. 'The last three digits—three, three, seven ... Once I punch them in, Melkur will be destroyed.' Then he drew back in consternation. 'But I can't complete the Sanction Program with the Doctor in there—it will destroy them both!'

Adric looked at him horror. 'And Nyssa and I have just sabotaged the Source Manipulator. It'll blow any minute!'

The Doctor found himself in a TARDIS. Not his own TARDIS, of course. The decor was in black, not white, and the shapes were subtly distorted. Standing at the console, was the horrifying figure of his oldest enemy.

The Doctor looked almost with sympathy at the loathsome figure in the tattered robes, remembering him in the days of his strength and pride. The stocky, powerful figure, the darkly handsome face with its pointed beard and burning eyes, the deep, hypnotic voice. All of that was gone, decayed, so that all that was left was a walking corpse.

But there was still a tinge of the old irony in the now-familiar voice. 'Well, Doctor?'

'Of course. I should have known. I think I did know really. The Master.'

The Master smiled. 'Welcome to my ship.'

'There's an ancient remedy for mad dogs, you know,' said the Doctor casually. 'I must look it up. Good library here, have you?'

'Unfortunately for you, you will not be using it, Doctor.'

The Doctor took a step towards him, and the Master flicked a switch. 'This whole domain is now keyed to my bio-rhythms, Doctor. Move a muscle and I shall destroy you.'

The Doctor found that he was quite unable to move.

By now the whole Chamber was ablaze with light, pulsing with swirls of violent energy.

118

Adric shook himself out of a horrified trance. 'Nyssa, the vault—we've got to disconnect.'

'We can't Adric, not at full power. It will be catastrophic!'

'But the Doctor ... it will destroy him!'

Slowly and painfully the Master hobbled over to his immobile captive. 'You will find immobility unpleasant but endurable, Doctor. I speak from experience.'

'I thought you were going to destroy me.'

'That would be irrational—a waste of the knowledge acquired over so many centuries. You spoke of my library, Doctor. I intend that you shall become part of it. I shall deposit your mind there. As for your body—I am now nearing the end of my twelfth regeneration.'

'And that is the end—even for a Time Lord.'

'But not for a Time Lord who is Keeper of Traken. With my new powers, much is possible.' The Master looked thoughtfully at the Doctor, rather like someone studying a suit of ready-made clothes upon a rack. 'Yes, I shall enjoy full mobility again.'

Suddenly a harsh wailing noise filled the Master's control room. He spun round, his face twisting with rage and fear. 'The Source! Someone is tampering with the Source!'

The Master scurried to the controls but as he touched them the whole console became alive with unleashed power.

The Master screamed, locked to the console by the energies surging through his wasted body.

The Doctor found he could move again. He searched for a way of escape, looking in puzzlement for a moment at the incongruous shape of the grandfather clock. The whole room seemed to pulse and shimmer around him and the Master's TARDIS seemed somehow insubstantial.

The room rocked with explosions and blazed with sheets of flame. Suddenly the Doctor dashed for one of the great vision screens and hurled himself through it.

Behind him the Master wrenched himself free of the console and dragged himself painfully towards the grandfather clock.

Great winds were swirling around the Sanctum now and the little group huddled together, waiting for the end. Luvic and Katura ran in to join them. Their guards had fled and they had instinctively sought the Sanctum, sensing the end was near. Tremas struggled towards the vault. Nyssa called. 'It's useless, father. You can't stop it now.'

'I must try,' shouted Tremas, and vanished inside.

Suddenly the Doctor materialised in the Chamber.

They ran towards him but the transparent doors were shut fast and refused to budge. The Doctor wrenched at them ...

From inside the Chamber they heard the Doctor's muffled voice. 'Three, three, seven. Key in the last three digits. Three, three, seven!'

Adric hurled himself across the Sanctum, forcing his way through the savage winds. Somehow he reached the console. Clinging on with one hand he punched up *three* ... another *three* ... A great gust of wind snatched him away from the console and sent him careering across the Sanctum.

With a desperate heave, the Doctor wrenched open the Chamber doors and staggered out into the Sanctum.

Step by step he made his way across the room, bent almost double, forcing his way through the almost solid force of the wind, his long scarf streaming out vertically behind him.

With a last desperate lunge he stabbed at the final seven ...

Suddenly everything was quiet.

The winds stopped, the fearful electronic howling stopped, and the lighting in the Sanctum returned to normal.

The Doctor went over to Adric and helped him up. 'Thank you, Adric. We seem to have cancelled out your little bit of sabotage—and put paid to the resident Keeper as well.'

They turned and saw Luvic and Katura staring at the Flame, which was sinking rapidly.

'The Flame dies,' whispered Katura fearfully.

The Doctor went over to them. 'I was going to mention that! If you want to keep the quaint old tradition of the Keeper going, I think someone should step rapidly into the breach.'

Katura and Luvic looked at each other. 'I am too old,' said Katura. 'You must go, Luvic.'

'But I am not worthy.'

'You must go!'

Luvic clasped her hands for a moment and then dashed into the Chamber.

The transparent walls closed around him, and he faded from sight.

Katura hurried to punch in the access code.

They waited anxiously—and the flame burned high.

Old Katura smiled. 'There was greatness in him after all.'

Tremas came bemusedly out of the vault and looked around him. 'What happened?'

Quickly the Doctor explained. 'It seems you've lost your chance of being Keeper once again, Tremas.'

Tremas said sadly, 'Just as my poor Kassia wanted.'

The Doctor nodded sympathetically. 'Still, I think you're lucky to have missed the job, on the whole.'

'I think we were all lucky, Doctor,' said Tremas solemnly. 'Lucky you came to Traken.'

'Ah well, I'm afraid that particular bit of luck has just run out,' said the Doctor in some embarrassment. 'It's time Adric and I were on our way.'

'That's right,' said Adric. 'We're supposed to be going to Gallifrey.'

'In a roundabout sort of way ... Come on, Adric, we must fly.'

He bustled Adric off.

The Doctor had always hated goodbyes.

Slinging hat, coat and scarf carelessly on the hatstand, the Doctor began a quick check of the TARDIS's flight systems. 'She seems to be right as ninepence now.'

'Why couldn't I start her up then?'

'One of the Master's little party tricks, I suppose.'

'This business with the Master – how did it all come about?'

The Doctor went on with his work. 'He needed energy, you see, energy to stay alive. He got some on Gallifrey, but it obviously wasn't enough ... So he planted himself close to one of the biggest energy sources in the cosmos, and bided his time.' The Doctor straightened up, and looked thoughtfully at the TARDIS console. 'Poor old thing needs a proper overhaul, really.'

'Why don't you do one, then?'

'Oh, there's an awful lot of detailed recalculation

involved,' said the Doctor vaguely. 'Never seem to find the time. Not really my forte, anyway.'

'You worked out the code for the Ultimate Sanction Program.'

'Oh that! Guesswork, mostly.'

'Still it worked.'

'Yes, it did, didn't it? Wouldn't it be nice to be right about everything!'

As the central column began its rise and fall, Adric said uneasily, 'I suppose the Master really was destroyed?'

'Well, he certainly ought to have been.' The Doctor smiled reminiscently. 'But with the Master, you can never be absolutely sure . . .'

Katura and Tremas stood looking around the Sanctum, now restored to peace and order once more. In the empty Chamber, the flame of the Source burned high. Katura gave a sigh of satisfaction. 'Now that the new Keeper is inaugurated, everything seems to be running properly again!'

Tremas smiled. 'Perhaps we can look forward to some peace at last.'

As Katura left the Sanctum, Nyssa appeared in the doorway. 'Come on, father, you'll be needed to put everything together again.'

'Starting with our quarters,' said Tremas wryly. 'I'll join you in a moment. Just one final check. Wait for me in the courtyard.'

Nyssa went off and Tremas took a last look around the room. He frowned as he caught sight of a strange object in an obscure corner of the Sanctum. It was tall and oblong with a round dial at the top.

He went over to examine it. There seemed to be some kind of door . . . Tremas reached out to touch it. A fierce current of energy ran through his body and he stood motionless, petrified.

The door opened and a hooded figure slipped out of the grandfather clock.

Thoughtfully the Master surveyed his paralysed victim. 'A new body at last!' It wasn't quite what he had planned – but it would serve. The Master had learned much from his brief contact with the Source. He stepped closer to Tremas and their bodies merged.

The Master disappeared – and Tremas changed.

He became younger, strong and upright. His hair changed from grey-streaked brown to glossy black, becoming shorter in the process and the straggling beard became black and sharp and pointed. The deep resonant voice said, 'Now begins my new life!'

The Master was himself again. He laughed, exulting in his new strength. He was free to roam the cosmos again, just like the Doctor.

Somewhere in space and time they would meet again.

The Master disappeared inside the clock and, with a strange wheezing groaning sound, the clock disappeared.

Nyssa came rushing back into the Sanctum 'Father, what's happening? Are you coming?'

Tremas was nowhere to be seen.

Nyssa shivered, looking round the empty Sanctum.

She seemed to hear the distant echo of mocking laughter.